"I've never had a day like this," she said. "Best of times and worst of times."

"Yeah? What was the best?" In his mind, he replayed their kiss by Teacup Lake.

"The autopsy, of course."

He should have guessed. "And the worst?"

"Being scared by the big bad Wolff."

He appreciated her sense of humor but knew she used jokes to deflect her real feelings. This woman didn't like being vulnerable. "I'm sorry that happened to you. If I'd been with you, Wolff never would have come close."

"True. You're definitely an alpha male."

"Can we be serious for a minute? I'd feel better if I could—with your permission—keep an eye on you."

"Like a bodyguard?"

Exactly like a bodyguard.

SHALLOW GRAVE

USA TODAY Bestselling Author

CASSIE MILES

To my New York family: Signe, Aaron and Finn. Can't wait to see you all. And, as always, to Rick.

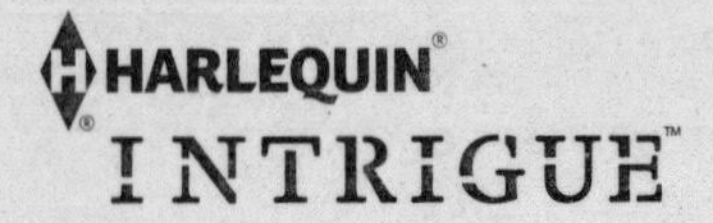

ISBN-13: 978-1-335-58323-9

Shallow Grave

For questions and comments about the quality of this book, please contact us at CustomerService@Harlequin.com.

Harlequin Enterprises ULC
22 Adelaide St. West, 41st Floor
Toronto, Ontario M5H 4E3, Canada
www.Harlequin.com

Printed in U.S.A.

Cassie Miles, a *USA TODAY* bestselling author, lived in Colorado for many years and has now moved to Oregon. Her home is an hour from the rugged Pacific Ocean and an hour from the Cascade Mountains—the best of both worlds—not to mention the incredible restaurants in Portland and award-winning wineries in the Willamette Valley. She's looking forward to exploring the Pacific Northwest and finding mysterious new settings for Harlequin Intrigue romances.

Books by Cassie Miles

Harlequin Intrigue

Mountain Retreat
Colorado Wildfire
Mountain Bodyguard
Mountain Shelter
Mountain Blizzard
Frozen Memories
The Girl Who Wouldn't Stay Dead
The Girl Who Couldn't Forget
The Final Secret
Witness on the Run
Cold Case Colorado
Find Me
Gaslighted in Colorado
Escape from Ice Mountain
Shallow Grave

Visit the Author Profile page at Harlequin.com.

CAST OF CHARACTERS

Daisy Brighton—While the high school anatomy teacher from Denver researches hidden outlaw treasure in mountain graveyards, she discovers evidence of a serial killer.

A. P. Carter—A National Park Service (NPS) ranger and investigator, he tracks down the killer using his knowledge and love of the mountains.

Violet Rhodes (Aunt Vi)—Daisy's vivacious sixty-eight-year-old aunt, who lives in Leadville.

The Good Guys—FBI agents Pat Wiley and Mickey Hicks, medical examiner Dr. Julia Sweetwater, and NPS director Joaquin Stanley.

Suspects—Jackknife Jones, Slade Franklin, and Eric and Gerald Wolff.

Victims—Rene Williams, Andrea Lindstrom, Hannah Guerrero and Eileen Findlay.

Chapter One

"Are we lost?"

"Not hardly." Jackknife Jones stuck his head out the window of his ramshackle truck and spat tobacco juice onto the two-lane gravel road. "Don't you worry your purty little head. I'll get you where you're going."

Daisy Brighton turned her head—which really wasn't all that purty or little—away from the grizzled old man behind the steering wheel and stared impatiently through the filthy windshield. Over an hour and a half ago when they'd left her aunt Violet Rhodes's house in Leadville, sunset had painted the skies above the Saguache Range in shades of magenta streaked by golden clouds and framed by blue spires of ponderosa pine and spruce. A snowy-white cloak draped over Mount Elbert, even though it was mid-June.

She'd expected to reach the cemetery before nightfall. *No such luck.* Obviously, Jackknife had no idea where he was going. Jostling on unpaved roads, the truck meandered and doubled back and circled around. Dusk had settled. Daisy was furious.

The headlight beam splashed across a boulder where someone had scrawled a heart and initials:

RAH + KB. She scowled. "Mr. Jones, I'm sure we already passed that graffiti."

"Like I told you, call me Jackknife." He cackled. "Don't let my name scare you."

It took more than a jackknife to frighten Daisy. For the past seven years, she'd taught high school biology in Denver, and a classroom full of teenagers was enough to strike terror into just about anybody, especially when she handed out scalpels for frog dissections.

Jackknife swerved the truck into an almost invisible right turn, and they continued to weave through San Isabel National Park and private property that was fenced off with barbed wire. They hadn't passed a town for miles.

She looked down at her cell phone. No bars. The GPS had quit working. No maps available. "You said the cemetery is near Butcher's Gulch, correct?"

"It's called a boot hill, sweet thang. Criminals and poor folks got buried there. Being left in a boot hill usually meant a violent death. These souls got kilt so fast they died with their boots on."

His description seemed apt for what she'd discovered from research into her ancestors—a motley collection of scoundrels, cheats, gunslingers and bandits. Her project over the summer break was to track down the final resting place for Sherwood Brighton, an outlaw who died in 1896. Her aunt believed her great-great-great-grandfather's grave would lead to the hiding place of his ill-gotten gains and had recruited Daisy to search. Already, she'd visited eight cemeteries.

"Just to be clear," she said. "You told Aunt Vi that you saw a grave marker in this boot hill cemetery with the name Brighton on it."

"You betcha." He tucked a fresh chaw of tobacco into his cheek. *Disgusting habit.* "Lemme ask you something about your auntie. Is she seeing anybody?"

"You mean dating?"

"I sure as heck do. Vi is a fine-looking woman."

Daisy wouldn't argue with that. Her aunt was tall and maintained her slim figure with daily exercise at the Leadville Yoga Center. The sun-streaked blond of her chin-length bob was dyed to match the color of Daisy's ponytail, and they both had green eyes. Vi was definitely stylish. Also, she was sixty-eight years old. Not that her age meant she couldn't have a boyfriend or two. But Daisy couldn't help feeling a twinge of irritation when she realized that Jackknife wanted her to play matchmaker. When was the last time a man had shown interest in Daisy? Here she sat on a Saturday night—date night—in a junky truck with a creep who'd offered to show her a cemetery.

"Violet doesn't have a steady guy," she muttered.

"Mebbe you could put in a good word for me."

Not going to happen. Her lips pinched together, holding back the obvious truth. No way would classy Vi go out with Jackknife unless he made some changes, starting with giving up tobacco. Also, he needed to shave the patchy whiskers. And it wouldn't hurt if he changed clothes and took a long, hot bath in industrial-strength disinfectant.

Still, she didn't want to alienate her ride home. Grudgingly, she said, "Maybe."

"Your auntie owns her house, right? She oughta have a man around to take care of her."

"Doesn't need a bodyguard. She's got a double-barreled shotgun."

"Does she have any other property? What about money in the bank?"

She gaped. Was this backwoods gigolo going after Vi for her money? Before she could tell him to back off, Daisy heard the discordant echo of electronic music. *In the middle of the forest?* The headlights shone on a sign for Butcher's Gulch Campground. "Finally! We're here."

"Nope, not yet," he said. "The ghost town is a coupla miles more, and then—"

"Stop. Right now." In a teacher voice that didn't allow for discussion, she gave the orders. "You're going to drive into the campground, where I can ask for directions."

Grumbling, he parked beside the Butcher's Gulch sign. "You shouldn't get out of the truck. Ain't safe."

"I can handle some kids playing their music too

loud." As if to emphasize her point, the volume lowered. "See. Not dangerous."

"The boot hill's haunted," he said. "And there's rumors of a man beast in a ski mask who attacks purty young girls like you."

Not wanting to argue until she got safely back to Leadville, she said nothing but got out of the truck, put on a denim jacket over her red cotton shirt and followed the gravel road that looped through a small campground. The two slots nearest the entrance provided parking for several vehicles, ranging from trucks and SUVs to a racy little sports car. She counted four tents and more than a dozen college-age people gathered around two fire pits. Some of them continued to dance to the tamped-down music while others guzzled beer from red plastic cups.

Asking the partygoers for directions seemed like a waste of time. This crew would be lucky to find their way to the outhouse in the middle of the night. She almost pivoted and returned to Jackknife's truck when she noticed a gunmetal-gray SUV with a National Park Service shield on the door. The tall man who reached for the door handle on the driver's side didn't wear the typical flat-brimmed hat, but he had a bison badge pinned to his dark green vest. A park ranger. He was exactly what she needed.

She approached him. "Excuse me."

The reflected blaze from the campfire flared in

his deep-set eyes and outlined the sharp edge of his jawbone, which contrasted with full, well-shaped lips. When he looked at her, he didn't smile, which was a bit disconcerting. "Can I help you?"

She met his unsmiling gaze with a toothy grin. "I'm looking for the Butcher's Gulch boot hill."

"Are you staying in this campground?"

"No."

"Coming to the party?" He gestured to the young people who barely looked old enough to drink but were carefully behaving within the limits of the law.

She widened her grin, probably causing him to wonder why she was so delighted to be searching for a cemetery. "You see, my ancestor is Sherwood Brighton, and I'm trying to find his grave. I'm Daisy Brighton."

He touched the brim of his weathered brown cowboy hat as he introduced himself. "I'm A. P. Carter. I go by Carter."

"Please call me Daisy." She nodded toward his badge. "You're a ranger."

"National Park Service, investigative services branch." Finally, he smiled. "And you're the heir to the legendary Brighton's Bullion."

"I am." She nodded, not surprised he'd heard the story of hidden treasure.

A pink-haired woman in skimpy cutoffs and combat boots sashayed toward them. She batted her super-long eyelashes at Carter. “What legend? Please tell me, Mr. Ranger.”

He lived up to Daisy’s expectations of an honorable park ranger when he put distance between himself and Pinkie. Though too young for the ranger and too drunk, she was clearly smitten. And who could blame her? Carter was a good-looking guy with a great smile when he chose to use it. He gave Daisy a nod. “Go ahead, Ms. Brighton, tell the story.”

“My ancestor, Sherwood Brighton, was an outlaw. In 1887, he pulled off a robbery on the Denver–Rio Grande Railroad.” Pinkie had already lost interest and scooted closer to Carter, which annoyed Daisy. Though the NPS ranger might not actually be her Saturday-night date, he could have been. At least, she was age appropriate at twenty-nine. He couldn’t be more than midthirties.

To get Pinkie’s attention, she used a teacher trick, waving a shiny object at the student. “Do you know how much a kilobar of gold bullion is worth?”

“A what?” Pinkie asked.

“Kilobar. It’s a brick, about two pounds of solid gold.”

“How big?” Pinkie held out the hand that wasn’t wrapped around a red plastic cup. “Could I hold it?”

“It’s about the same size as a paperback book. One kilobar is worth about $56,000 at today’s rates.

Sherwood Brighton stole fifty of them. He got away, and the bullion was never found." The math, she suspected, would be beyond Pinkie. "Fifty kilobars at fifty-six thou each. That's $2.8 million."

"No way." Pinkie downed her beer with one glug, straightened her shoulders and motioned to the others. "Hey, we've got to look for the kilobars."

Carter leaned close and said, "Should I give her the bad news or will you?"

"Let me." Daisy waited until the dancers and drinkers gathered around. "Brighton's Bullion has been missing since 1887. Hundreds have searched. No one has found it." Which was why she had no problem telling the story.

"I wish you luck on the search." Carter stepped forward and addressed the party-goers. "In the meantime, you people need to keep the music low, watch your fires and don't drive drunk. If I get another complaint about disorderly conduct and have to come here again, tickets will be issued and some of you will be taken into custody."

When they started to complain, he slashed his hand and cut off their voices. "That's final."

"Excuse me," Daisy said. "Directions to the boot hill?"

He took her arm, escorted her to the passenger side of his vehicle and opened the door. "Might be easier if I take you there."

She was about to regretfully refuse when she glanced toward the entry sign. The truck was gone. Jackknife had dumped her without transportation in the middle of San Isabel National Park. Though justifiably ticked off, she wouldn't complain. The old tobacco chewer's indifference resulted in her riding with Ranger A. P. Carter, which had to be pure serendipity. Cheerfully, she climbed into his SUV.

"Where did you park your vehicle?" he asked.

"At my aunt's house where I'm staying in Leadville."

"You're a long way from home." His smile dissolved, and he regarded her with the same kind of authoritative hostility that had silenced the pesky campers. "How did you get here?"

"I caught a ride with a friend of my aunt. We got lost, and when I saw the sign for the campground, I wanted to stop and ask for directions. He must have taken off."

"Not much of a friend. Come with me."

Carter's SUV had been kept in tip-top condition, ensuring a smooth ride, a quiet engine and precisely controlled temperature, but she couldn't relax. Daisy didn't like his disapproving attitude. She wasn't a flake and had never been a troublemaker. The opposite, in fact—she was the sort of woman who solved problems and was prepared for crises. Even now, when she might have been helpless and stranded, she'd thought to bring her cell phone and had a wallet with twenty bucks and a credit card in her pocket. It might be too far to get back to Leadville tonight, but she could manage.

When he looked toward her, she studied his face in the glow from the dashboard. His eyes were bright blue, and his hair was black. His smile had disappeared. "You're not a happy camper."

"Don't worry, Ms. Brighton. I'll make sure you get home in one piece."

"Call me Daisy."

"Okay… Daisy. Now, what's the procedure when we get to the cemetery?"

"I find markers and read names. Some are carved in stone. Others are faded scribbles on weathered wood. Many of the old cemeteries have undergone restoration, which means the graves are neatly outlined with stones and the inscriptions displayed clearly." The tombstones often left poignant epitaphs, such as "lynched and deserved it" or "trampled in stampede, died too young" or "stabbed by heartless wife."

"What led you here?" he asked. "What is it about this particular boot hill?"

"The guy who abandoned me said he saw a marker with Brighton written on it. Don't know if I can believe him, but it's worth a look."

Carter tapped the brake and brought the SUV to a near stop before bumping off the road and over the shoulder onto a track through high grasses and sagebrush. After about fifty yards, he parked and announced, "Welcome to Butcher's Gulch."

Before she left the SUV, he handed her an extra flashlight from the glove compartment. Outside, she noticed more of a chill in the air and fastened two buttons on her denim jacket. Her imagination cranked into high gear as she approached the ruins of the ghost town. The beam of her flashlight slid up and down a stone fireplace attached to a crumbling stone wall. A window without glass stood above the rickety planks of a porch. The ruins of what might have been a main street formed a line on one side. There was another fireplace. And a broken-down wagon with a busted wheel. A tire swing hung from a low tree branch.

Her gaze lifted, and she looked up at a million diamond-bright stars and a quarter moon. Whatever life energy populated Butcher's Gulch had scattered on the summer breeze and vanished in the pine-scented mountain air. She didn't believe in ghosts but felt the presence of memories. Long ago, these tumbledown houses had been filled with laughter and the sounds of children singing. Families had embraced. Lovers had kissed. But there had also been tears and tragedies. A shiver constricted the muscles in her neck. Had there been fear? Were there screams that slashed through the night?

WALKING SLOWLY AND enjoying the cool summer night, Carter came up beside Daisy. When he touched her shoulder, she reacted with a shiver.

Her face tilted up toward his, and her gaze flickered as though afraid to settle too long and become trapped.

"Something wrong?" he asked.

"I had an illogical premonition of danger."

"Not so odd. We're on our way to a boot hill."

"But I don't believe in superstition. I'm a scientist—a biology teacher."

"Science can't explain everything."

Being a ranger, alone in the national parks for many hours per week, he'd learned to prepare for the exceptions rather than trust in the rules. Mother Nature was an unpredictable old broad. Just when he thought he had things figured out, his expectations would be turned upside down. When he set out tonight, he'd never thought he'd meet a woman with the cheerful name of Daisy Brighton who was looking for a gold bullion in a graveyard. Never thought he'd be attracted to her wide, confident smile and her irritation when she tucked messy strands of her curly blond hair behind her ear. He liked that she was an organized woman and got a kick out of how annoyed she seemed when things got out of hand. She'd be fun to tease.

With his flashlight, he pointed downhill toward a tumbledown stone wall surrounding a clearing at the edge of the forest. "That's the boot hill over there."

"How do you know?"

"I've been here before. That's what park rangers

do. We range. And we explore. The campground is only a mile from here through those trees." Again, he used the beam of his flashlight as a pointer. "Listen."

She went silent and appeared to concentrate. "I hear it. Do you have to go back and shut down the party?"

"Not yet. I told them they could play their music until ten thirty."

Taking care of drunk and disorderly campers wasn't his usual job as an investigator, but Carter had added an extra layer of vigilance, personally checking out every complaint. A couple of people reported a Peeping Tom, some guy in a ski mask. It was his job to protect those who came to enjoy nature—the innocent hikers, sightseers and campers. He glanced at Daisy and added treasure hunters to his list.

She swooped her flashlight in a circle. "I think I see a marker over there to the left. I'll hike down and take a closer look."

"I'll start at the opposite side," he said. "We can meet in the middle."

Ambient light from the moon and stars helped him find his way to the remnants of a low stone wall. Four ponderosa pines loomed over the graves at the northern edge. Shrubs and high grasses had taken over much of the cemetery. He found a cluster of weathered wooden crosses with the names rewritten in black lettering. These four graves were occupied by the same outlaw gang.

He called out to her, "Are you okay?"

"I'm a lot better off than this guy whose marker says he was killed by a moose."

He moved closer to the trees and heard the rippling from a creek. He crinkled his nose. The night breeze carried a rotten stench. He might be having a premonition of his own. When he peered into the forest, he saw a reflection from the watching eyes of a nocturnal predator, probably a coyote or a wolf. Why would a night hunter lurk so close to humans? He unsnapped the safety strap on his belt holster, making it easier to draw his Beretta if it became necessary.

Looking down, he saw that someone had gone to the trouble of outlining a grave site with stones. Carter took care to walk around the edges rather than stepping on a final resting place. He was probably more superstitious than Daisy.

Before walking to the middle of the boot hill, he returned to the north edge to make sure he'd seen everything. Beside a clump of chokecherries, he found an open grave. Shallow, it couldn't have been more than five inches deep. The woman who lay supine on the overturned soil had been dead long enough to attract predators. Her flesh was torn. Half her face was gone. The blood on her clothing had dried to ugly brown stains. In the moonlight, her skin took on a gray-blue tint, deeper in places from bruising. The stench of putrefied flesh clogged his nostrils. He saw a wound at her neck that was partially covered by a flowing silk scarf.

Two weeks ago, he'd seen another body laid out and similarly displayed at a graveyard in Glenwood Springs. Her name was Hannah Guerrero. She'd also worn a scarf.

"Carter, come here." Daisy's voice trembled. "Hurry. I found a woman. She's dead."

A third victim.

According to the FBI, three murders meant they were looking for a serial killer.

Chapter Two

In the boot hill, at the edge of the forest, Daisy crouched beside the body of a woman lying on the ground with her legs stretched out. Her flashlight lay beside her with the beam shining through the tall grass toward stone and wooden markers. Aware that the young woman was very likely dead and should be left untouched for the CSI investigators, Daisy was compelled to feel for a pulse. Her flesh felt cold. A delicate butterfly tattoo floated above her wrist. No pulse.

The onset of rigor mortis had tightened her muscles and caused her jaw to clench. Her eyelids squeezed shut. Her long, straight brown hair fanned out around her face. A pretty face, not peaceful in death but tense and somehow frightened.

The person who had arranged the body—the murderer—had taken care with her, making sure the buttons on her blouse were fastened and her khaki slacks weren't bunched or wrinkled. Bright red blood glistened on the wound that slashed across her throat. A long, flower-patterned silk scarf tied around her neck obscured most of the laceration. The freshness of the blood made Daisy wonder if the killer was still nearby.

She peeked over her shoulder and peered into the deep, dark forest. Anyone could be hiding there.

Cougars, coyotes and bears, oh my. Again, she called out, "I need you, Carter."

"I'm on my way."

She placed the woman's hand across her flat stomach, where it had been before. "I'm so sorry," Daisy whispered. She didn't believe the dead woman could hear her words but wanted to show respect. "I hope your life was well lived."

Though adrenaline pumped through her, Daisy didn't experience feelings of shock or fear. This wasn't her first dead body. When she was in high school taking an advanced placement biology class, she'd been lucky enough to share a cadaver with other students. Since then, she'd seen other corpses in college-level classes or at the body farm where she studied forensic anatomy.

She stood and picked up her flashlight. Newly killed, this victim was unique in her experience. Daisy wiped the nervous sweat from her forehead. Facing this dead woman disturbed her more than studying a medically prepared body laid out on an examination table. Surely, there was something she could learn. Slowly and deliberately, she directed the beam from the top of the woman's head to the scarf and death wound, then down her body to her feet, which were bare. Leaning down, she inspected the soles. Not dirty at all.

As Carter approached, she noticed that he walked in a zigzag pattern to avoid stepping on graves. *Superstitious?* When he came close, his flashlight beam shone on her, then the body, then back to her. "I'll be damned. Another one."

"What do you mean?"

"On the other side of the cemetery, I stumbled across a shallow grave. Another dead woman."

"A serial killer?"

"Could be." Though she couldn't see his eyes under his cowboy hat, she felt his gaze assessing her as he said, "You seem calm. Doesn't this upset you?"

"Of course it does. Murder is a terrible thing. But…"

"What?"

"I teach biology, and I usually get cadavers for my students. Those bodies are medically prepped for us to study, but they're still dead people."

"Uh-huh."

"And I've also taken classes and worked at the body farm outside Denver, where the dead are buried in different conditions and left for students to study. The smell there is—well, it's something else."

"Uh-huh."

"Anyway, I don't believe this woman was killed at this location. Look here—you can see that her bare feet are clean. She didn't walk through the forest or the grass."

He leaned down to see. In the reflected glow of the flashlight, she noticed that his skin had paled under his tan. His lips pinched tightly together in the tense expression of a person who was holding on to self-control with both hands to keep from losing it.

"Good observation," he said in a coarse voice. "You're right about the feet."

His squeamish reaction surprised her. She'd figured that—in his work as a ranger—he was either a hunter or familiar with their procedures, like field dressing and skinning an elk, which was way more gruesome than this. Also, since he worked as an investigator, he'd certainly seen dead bodies before. "Sorry, Carter. I didn't mean to gross you out."

"I'm fine." He pointed his flashlight up the hill. "Walk with me. I need to go to my car and radio headquarters for backup support."

"Doesn't your cell phone work?"

"Reception is spotty around here." He took a couple of backward steps and waited for her to do the same before hiking toward the ghost town.

For a moment, they walked without speaking. The crunching sound of their footsteps on dry pine needles mingled with other noises—the distant echo of music from the campground, the breeze whispering through the pine boughs and the incessant skittering of nocturnal creatures. And killers. Was he close? Had he been watching them?

Carter hadn't asked for her opinion but hadn't told her to pipe down. She volunteered another comment. "If I had to make an educated guess,

I'd say time of death was no more than three hours ago, probably more like two."

"Why is that?"

"The blood at her throat is fresh, rigor mortis is just starting to set in and there's minimal evidence of flies, maggots or animal predators."

"I've got to tell you, Daisy, you're not what I expected." He stopped beside the broken-down chimney at the edge of Butcher's Gulch, took off his hat and raked his fingers through his thick black hair. "I thought you were a city woman visiting her auntie and poking around at Western history. After a couple of weeks, I figured you'd be bored and run back to Denver."

She had to admit that he wasn't altogether wrong. "I'm not deeply invested in the search for Brighton's Bullion. But my aunt Vi is my last living relative, and I care about her enough to make the effort."

"There's something more to your visit than spending time with family," he said. "You were drawn to the mountains. You're not panicky about finding a body because you consider death to be natural. You aren't nervous about coyotes or bears."

She wasn't sure if he was complimenting her or making fun of her. "What are you trying to tell me, Carter?"

"I'm saying you fit in. You're comfortable here."

"Maybe or maybe not. I've always lived in the city." Every morning she awoke with the sun and happily greeted the majestic outline of the front range of the Rockies from her bedroom window, but she had no desire to come here like a pioneer and settle into a log cabin. "Did you grow up in the mountains?"

"I was a cop in Denver before I became a ranger." He replaced the hat on his head. "I love my job, and I'm usually good at it. I kind of hate that I got queasy. And that you pointed it out. You're a little bit pushy."

"Guilty." As if she needed his approval.

"I'm not judging."

"No?"

"I like you, Daisy."

His statement was simple, direct and totally charming. It took a confident man to leave himself so vulnerable. What if she shot him down? Or the opposite, she might take his comment as an invitation to sex. Confused, she said, "Thank you?"

"I appreciate your intelligence, and I'd be a damn fool if I didn't take advantage of your expertise. What else can you tell me about the dead woman?"

Relieved, she returned to a topic she knew something about. "When I first arrived, I took her hand to feel for a pulse. I noticed her fingernail polish was chipped, and one nail was torn. Makes me think that she fought for her life."

"Anything else?"

"There was a strange smell. Not the typical aromas I associate with the dead."

"I noticed it, too," he said. "Bear repellent. I don't put much stock in dousing your campsite with weird combinations of ammonia, garlic, sulfur and other stuff, but there are people who swear it will keep the animals and the insects away."

She made the logical assumption. "The killer must have used repellent because he didn't want predators to damage her body. That fits with the way he arranged her and fixed her hair."

"And tied a scarf around her throat. The other body also had a scarf. I wonder why." He frowned. "Maybe it'd be useful to consult a profiler."

A profiler? Talking with that type of expert could be extremely interesting. In spite of her respect for the dead woman, Daisy felt a glimmer of selfish excitement. She could be part of a murder investigation. *Cool!*

Headlights flashed behind Carter's SUV as Jackknife's beat-up truck pulled up and parked. The old man jumped out, spat tobacco juice, waved his scrawny arm and hollered, "Howdy, sweet thang. I'm back. Bet you're glad to see me."

Carter aimed his flashlight into the grizzled face. "Stop right there."

When the beam hit Jackknife, he squinted. "You got a problem, sonny boy?"

"NPS Ranger Carter," he identified himself. "Show me your registration and license."

"It's okay," Daisy assured him. "This is Mr. Jones. He drove me here."

"And left you without a ride. Not a real nice guy." His flashlight didn't waver. "I need your identification."

The old man spat again. "If'n I don't feel like showing it, what's gonna happen?"

With lightning speed, Carter flipped his flashlight to his left hand. With his right, he drew his Beretta. "Hands on top of your head, Jones. I don't have time to play games."

If Jackknife considered fighting back, that notion disappeared when Carter took a determined step toward him. The ranger wasn't goofing around, and Jackknife knew it. He put both hands on top of his John Deere cap with the leaping stag logo. "I'll do whatever you say, Ranger. I'll cooperate."

In a few efficient moves, Carter cuffed Jackknife with his hands in front, took his car keys and helped him climb into the driver's seat of his truck. "Stay here until I have time to take your statement."

"Statement about what? What the heck is going on here?"

"Murder investigation," Carter said.

"Somebody got killed?" His voice creaked into a higher octave. "I don't know nothing about it. Tell him, Daisy."

She opened her mouth to speak, but before she could get a word out, Jackknife continued, "And what about her, huh? If'n I can't drive, how's she gonna get home?"

"I'll arrange for her ride," Carter said.

"I couldn't ask you to do that now," she said, not wanting to be a bother in the middle of an investigation. "It's a long way back to Leadville."

"What are you talking about?" He shot her a puzzled glance. "It's only about forty minutes—less because there's no traffic or snow."

"Only forty minutes, huh?" She glared at Jackknife. "We were in your truck for more than twice that long."

"Mebbe I got lost."

More likely, he was playing a joke on her. *Not funny.* "I suggest you get comfortable in that rattletrap truck, because Ranger Carter has a lot of work to do before he talks to you."

She turned her back on him and strode toward the NPS vehicle.

Carter came up beside her. "How well do you know that guy?"

"Not well at all."

"Do you have any reason to suspect him?"

She couldn't believe her aunt would let her get into the truck with Jackknife if she thought he was up to no good. But Aunt Vi wouldn't count this grungy, tobacco-spitting old man as a friend. "He's kind of a jerk but probably harmless."

"That's how the neighbors of serial killers always describe them. They always say that the monster was harmless, a nice guy who kept to himself and wouldn't hurt a fly."

She reconsidered. If her time-of-death analysis was accurate, Jackknife could have murdered that woman and returned to Leadville before he picked her up. They were on the road for over an hour and a half before they got close to Butcher's Gulch. Why would Jackknife purposely delay? Why would he drive around in circles? A possible answer hit her—he might have been waiting for darkness to fall.

He might have planned a murder scenario for her. Shivers scampered across her back like a herd of spiders. "Jackknife Jones could be the killer."

"Jackknife, huh? I don't even want to guess how he got that nickname." Carter opened the driver's side door of his car. "I'll be with you in a minute. I need to put through a call to headquarters."

She had a similar thought. Her aunt deserved a call so she wouldn't worry, but Daisy's cell phone still didn't have reception. Earlier when they were driving to Butcher's Gulch in Carter's SUV, she'd noticed a bunch of screens and communication devices attached to the center console, including a heavy-looking phone on a charger—a satellite phone, too bulky to carry in your pocket but essential in areas without good access to cell phone towers.

Standing just outside the open driver's side door, she watched as he took that phone rather than using his police radio that would alert anyone listening on that open line. Apparently, he wanted privacy when he talked to headquarters.

"Excuse me," she said. "Can I use your sat phone to call my aunt?"

"When I'm done." Taking the phone with him, he left the car, locked the door and started back toward the boot hill. "Come with me. Stay close."

Further warning was unnecessary. She'd seen the murdered woman and knew there was a killer at large. If not Jackknife, then who? There didn't seem to be anyone living in this area. When she scanned the forested hills and rocky cliffs, she didn't see house lights. Could they have come from the campground?

She half listened while Carter rattled off instructions to NPS headquarters. He wanted assistance from the local sheriff's office, the state highway patrol and agents from the FBI. He repeated "FBI" twice and added, "Tell them we're looking for a serial killer. They need to arrange for the autopsies."

Plural—as in more than one. She shuddered and fidgeted. Though she stayed close to Carter, Daisy wandered through the graves, shining her flashlight beam on the markers. This side of the cemetery featured several fieldstone markers with names roughly chiseled and occasional embellishments, usually angels or hearts and flowers. Daisy tripped over a chunk of granite that was almost completely obscured by the high grasses. Kneeling, she lowered her flashlight beam and read the inscription: "Annie Brighton. Wife, Friend and Lover."

There was no date of birth or death. No indication of what killed her. But Daisy knew she'd found the final resting place of Sherwood Brighton's wife.

Chapter Three

Ranger A. P. Carter ended his call to Joaquin Stanley, his supervisor at the National Park Service headquarters in Salida, and hiked through the graves to where Daisy knelt beside a tombstone. She shook her flashlight at a rugged stone, causing the beam to flicker. "Read it."

"'Annie Brighton. Wife, Friend and Lover.'" He wasn't thinking about treasure hunting. Not now. The double—no, triple—murder investigation would be hell to coordinate among the several law enforcement jurisdictions and would take his full attention. "Is this good news or bad?"

"It's unexpected. I was looking for Sherwood, not his wife, and I don't know much about her. Also, this marker is sort of vindication for Jackknife. He wasn't lying about seeing the name in the Butcher's Gulch boot hill."

"Don't be so quick to forgive. There's no explanation for why he pretended to be lost."

"I'm not defending him. Jackknife is a total jerk but probably not be a serial killer." She shrugged. "May I use your sat phone to call my aunt? She'll be pleased about finding Annie."

"First, there's something I want your opinion on." He hooked the sat phone onto his belt. "The county sheriff has been alerted, and his deputies will arrive soon. When they do, I won't be able to talk with you."

"Why? Am I going to disappear?"

"You're a civilian, Daisy. Some of these guys will try to shove you out of the way. They won't understand or accept your expertise, but I do." Holding her slender hand, he led her down the hill, hoping he wasn't making a mistake by recruiting a high school biology teacher as a consultant. "I want you to take a look at this shallow grave."

"Where is she?"

"Down this slope."

He'd debated with himself before trusting her. Though he appreciated her straightforward analysis of the other victim, he couldn't get around the fact that she wasn't a cop or a ranger or a medical examiner. He had hesitated because sharing the details of a murder smacked of unprofessional behavior. But what the hell should he do? This case was different. He'd never investigated a serial murder and had never faced the possibility of more victims being attacked if he didn't solve it quickly. Carter needed all the help he could get.

Walking slowly behind him, she pinched her nose. "This one has been dead long enough for the flesh to putrefy."

"How long is that?"

"At least three days."

Knowing the medical details before the deputies showed up gave Carter an edge. While they were gagging and puking in the forest, he could plan the strategy for his investigation. The timing of the murders—especially when combined with what he'd seen of Hannah Guerrero in Glenwood Springs—was an important factor. He rubbed at his nose, trying to erase the stench. "You know, Daisy, if you don't want to go any farther, it's okay."

"I don't mind the smell. When I was working at the body farm, I got used to it." She kept moving forward. "I'd like to ask a favor from you."

"Go ahead."

"I've never seen an actual autopsy. Can you arrange for me to watch?"

For the life of him, he couldn't figure out why he was attracted to this woman. "I can arrange for you to sit in."

Her thank-you and enthusiastic smile would have been appropriate for someone who'd been given freebie tickets on the fifty-yard line for a Denver Broncos playoff game. "Where will it take place?"

"That's up to the FBI," he said. "I'm guessing Pueblo."

At the edge of the shallow grave, he forced himself to, once again, look down at the dead woman whose clothing was ripped and bloodstained. What was left of her face appeared to be bloated, and her discolored flesh had turned a dead gray color.

Daisy crouched and slid the beam of her flashlight up and down the body. "It's hard to believe this is the handiwork of the same killer. The other woman was handled delicately, while this one looks like she was abused. The only item of clothing that appears to be clean is the long scarf around her neck. Do you see the bruises on her arms and ligature marks on her wrists? She might have been tied down. If you call in a profiler, they could draw a lot of inferences from this."

"I'll make sure we have photos of both bodies." He hadn't been so diligent with the Glenwood corpse. Not his jurisdiction. Not his case. But Daisy was correct. A profiler would add a different perspective, especially when studying similarities among the victims. They were all young and fit, average height and weight. Their coloring was different. Hannah Guerrero had black hair and olive skin. The woman Daisy found had long brown hair. This one was platinum blonde. The killer didn't seem to have a preferred type. "What else?"

Using a stick she found on the ground, Daisy lifted the hand and showed him the limp wrist. "She's already gone through rigor, and the stiffness has worn off. Like I said, time of death was probably over two or three days ago."

"Can you narrow it down?"

"Not with precision," she said. "Body temp won't be a good indicator because she's been outdoors, and temperature at this time of year fluctuates by several degrees from day to night. And I don't have a liver thermometer."

He wished real-life forensics could be as clear

and infallible as portrayed on television. Hannah had been killed in Glenwood ten days ago. If this woman had been dead for three days, that meant a seven-day difference before he killed a second time. The body that Daisy found was recently murdered, which meant the interim had grown shorter.

Without hesitation, Daisy leaned close and aimed the flashlight beam at the dead woman's horribly mangled face. "Maggots. Do you see the eggs?"

Carter looked into the wound. Small, pale eggs mingled with crawly insects. "I see them." He gagged. This was as close as he'd come to vomiting at a murder scene. He would have preferred being stoic, but his nausea occurred as an automatic reflex.

"There isn't too much damage by predators. Torn clothes. Teeth and claw marks here and there. I suspect there was something shielding her body." She sat back on her heels and looked up at him. "Or she might have been murdered somewhere else. He might have allowed the blood to drain before bringing her to this shallow grave."

"Can you tell how much she bled onto the dirt below her?"

"Not without moving the body," she said, "and I don't think your medical examiner would appreciate that much interference. Also, I can't turn her to check on lividity—the way the blood settled after death."

So many questions, and he needed to find answers to all of them. If there had been something covering her and shielding her from local predators, he needed to search. If she'd been held somewhere else, he might find that the killer lived in the area. Or he could have loaded the dead woman in his car and brought her here.

He started a mental checklist: Check for tire tracks. Search for something that covered the body. Look for a shovel or spade. Search the forest in this area. So much to do and so little time before he handed over jurisdiction of the investigation.

AFTER DAISY MADE her phone call to Aunt Vi and returned the sat phone to Carter, she heard the wail of a police siren bouncing off the canyon walls. Together, she and Carter hiked up the gently sloping hill to the ghost town and greeted the deputies who emerged from an SUV with the county sheriff's logo on the door. Though she stood ready and willing to help, the two officers—Graham and Escobar—barely acknowledged her presence. Carter had predicted that she'd be ignored as a mere civilian, and he'd been correct.

Not being a person who demanded a lot of attention, she was glad to step back and quietly observe what was happening. Deputy Graham—a clean-shaven, athletic-looking man in a dark green uniform and a baseball cap with the county logo—brightened when Carter told them they might be dealing with a serial killer. He immediately covered his unacceptable grin with a scowl, but she'd seen his excitement, and she understood. Serial killers were strange and terrifying creatures. Legendary, like boogiemen or vampires, they haunted nightmares and struck fear in the hearts of average citizens. Tracking one down meant a major challenge for a young deputy in a mainly rural county.

Carter asked, "Do you have lights for the crime scene?"

"Sure do," Graham replied as he hooked his thumbs in his belt on either side of a shiny rodeo championship buckle for bronc riding.

"How about some of those throwaway booties so we don't mess up footprints?"

"I got those and latex gloves, too."

"Let's gather the gear and set up at the location of the first body."

"There's more than one." Graham stated the obvious description of a serial killer. "Are they all in the graveyard?"

"Two are here. Ten days ago, there was a third." Carter turned to the other deputy, a middle-aged guy wearing the uniform shirt with weathered jeans and boots. "I'd appreciate if you stay here and meet the others who have been contacted."

Cool and casual, Deputy Escobar nodded. "We'll have another vehicle from our office. And I expect you contacted the NPS, so there will be a couple of rangers. Who else?"

"State patrol, coroner, ambulance and FBI.

Could be more than that. My supervisor made the calls." Carter matched the calm, controlled attitude of the older lawman. "I don't want a herd of investigators trooping through the graveyard messing up evidence. If you need more information about what we're dealing with, you can talk with Ms. Brighton."

She straightened her shoulders, glad to be helpful, and gave a small wave to the deputy. Escobar signaled for her to come closer. "Want some coffee, Brighton?"

"Call me Daisy. And yes on the coffee."

He led her to the passenger side of the SUV, pulled out a long silver thermos and poured hot liquid into a disposable cup. "I hope you like it black. My wife sends me out the door with plenty of sandwiches and strong coffee when I'm on night shift."

"Black is perfect." She sipped. Even though the coffee wasn't delicious, she knew the caffeine would lift her spirits. "Thanks, Deputy. Do you have any questions?"

He leaned against the front bumper of his vehicle and watched as Carter and the younger deputy gathered equipment from the back. "What were you doing in the graveyard?"

"Research," she said as though it was the most normal thing in the world to be poking around in a graveyard after dark. "Carter was kind enough to help me, and I found the first body."

"That must have scared you."

"Not at all."

She rattled through an explanation about being a biology teacher who regularly handled cadavers and segued into forensic descriptions of the two murdered women. Occasionally, Escobar asked questions, and she answered as best she could.

She had a question of her own. "Have you worked with Carter before?"

"A couple of times. He's a good man." He tasted his coffee and slanted a wise glance in her direction. "You like him."

"I didn't say that."

"Didn't need to. Your eyes did the talking." He grinned. "And why not? You two go together like peanut butter and jelly. You're both smart and good-looking. You're both concerned about other folks."

"How do you figure?"

"He's a ranger. You're a teacher. Caretakers."

"There's nothing going on between me and Carter."

She truly wished relationships could be as simple as matching a few personality traits, but she'd never found attraction to be easy, and she hadn't really had enough time to analyze the possibilities. Of course, she found Carter to be physically appealing. He was tall and lean and looked like the romantic archetype of a cowboy in his hat, boots and jeans. The curly black hair, expressive eyes and great smile were additional pluses. If she'd been younger, she might have jumped into a brief fling with the ranger, but she was twenty-nine and ready for something more than a quickie—as Aunt Vi would say, "a roll in the hay." Daisy wanted to settle down, get serious and start a family.

Nothing long-term would work between her and Carter. He was a mountain man. And she was a city woman.

She was saved from further embarrassing conversation with Escobar by the arrival of three vehicles: one from the park service, another from the county sheriff and a patrol car with the Colorado state logo on the door and red and blue flashers whirring on the roof. The officers, rangers and deputies gathered around while Escobar told them to stay put until Carter came back up the hill and explained the situation. "He doesn't want y'all tromping around and messing up the evidence." Escobar craned his neck, scanning the group. "I don't suppose there's a coroner here."

"We heard this was a serial killer," one of the state police officers said.

The two rangers complained that this was really their crime scene, and they needed to be with Carter. There was more grumbling all around.

"Settle down," Escobar said. "Ms. Brighton, would you mind heading down to the site and telling Carter to come up here?"

She was delighted to walk away from the impatient crew of rangers and officers. Though she'd already made a couple of trips through the graveyard, she still needed her flashlight until she got close to where Carter and Graham had positioned two portable, battery-operated units that spotlighted the scene like a movie set. Though she saw more details, the body looked as unreal as the plastic cadavers she sometimes used for her classes.

Graham stood as far away from the dead woman as possible without disappearing into the shadows while Carter got in close and personal to inspect the fatal wound at her throat. His queasiness seemed to have diminished. He waved her over. "Daisy, take a look at this."

When she leaned down beside him, she caught a whiff of the mentholated gel that was supposed to mask the stink of bear repellent and death. Graham must have brought it. "What did you want to show me?"

With latex gloves covering both hands, he gently separated the scarf from the blood. "There are already insect eggs."

"Blowflies," she said. "They're drawn by the smell of carrion and show up immediately."

He ordered the deputy to make sure he took close-up photos. To her, he said, "There's a crowd gathering at the top of the hill."

"That's why I'm interrupting you. Escobar could use some help dealing with them."

"Has the FBI arrived?"

"Not yet," she said. "Why do you ask?"

"With their state-of-the-art databases and forensic equipment, they typically assume jurisdiction on serial murders. I need to talk to the feds before I hand over control."

"It doesn't seem fair for you to just step aside."

"What's fair is finding the killer before he strikes again," he said as he stood. "You're not wearing your booties."

"My bad." She rose tilted her head to gaze into his vivid blue eyes. This was the first time she'd gotten a good look at him in clear light, and she wasn't disappointed. The spotlights for the crime scene reflected off his high cheekbones and the smile that hid his true nature as a sharp, decisive man. Was that also a trait they shared? She suspected it was. She and Carter were both people who got things done.

Whoops and laughter resonated from the thick pine forest beyond boot hill. She saw Pinkie step away from the trees followed by several others from the party at the campground. They were about a hundred yards away.

Carter whirled and started toward them. "Daisy, come with me. Graham, go up to the top of the hill and tell the crew that one person from each vehicle can come down here."

"They need to wear gloves and booties," Graham said.

"Make sure they do. That's your responsibility."

Daisy followed as he marched toward the raucous partygoers, who must have followed the path from the campground. The woman with pink hair appeared to be their leader. She gave an enthusiastic but sloppy-drunk wave. "Hey there, Mr. Ranger. What's with all the cop cars?"

"There's an investigation underway." Carter continued to stride toward them. Even in his baby blue paper booties, he exuded authority.

"Cool!" Pinkie said. "What kind of investigation?"

As they approached the group of five people, Daisy recognized some of them from the party—three men, Pinkie and one other woman with red hair in two ponytails. One of the guys seemed totally wasted, but the other two were alert. The tallest, a husky guy with a buzz cut, looked a bit older than the others, maybe in his early thirties. He explained, "We heard the sirens and wanted to find out what was going on."

"That's her." Pinkie jabbed her index finger in Daisy's direction. "She's the lady who's a treasure hunter."

"Brighton's Bullion," said the tall guy. "Had any luck?"

"Not really." No point in telling him about Sherwood's wife's grave.

The other relatively sober guy squinted through horn-rimmed glasses and tried to step around Carter. "There's lights set up over there. It looks like a body on the ground."

With his arms spread wide, Carter herded them back toward the trail. "I need you to stay out of the way."

"Is he right?" Pinkie asked. "Was somebody murdered?"

"Yes." Carter dropped his arms. "And you're witnesses. I need information from—"

"Wait a minute." Her eyelids twitched, and she looked like she was going to cry. "Is she about my height? Does she have brown hair?"

"Yes."

"And a tattoo?" Pinkie said. "A butterfly tattoo on her left wrist."

Daisy couldn't help nodding when Pinkie looked toward her.

"Oh my God." Pinkie sobbed. "It's Rene."

Chapter Four

Carter hated the disorganized way this investigation was unfolding. Even if he didn't have the jurisdiction to hunt a serial killer, he'd hoped to hand over a coherent package of evidence to the FBI agents instead of a jumbled mess. From literally stumbling over the bodies to having a half-drunk, pink-haired woman blurt out the identity of the victim, every bit of information had come in random, unexpected bursts. Nothing—with the exception of Daisy's forensic observations—had been the result of logic or intelligent discovery. He needed to step up and take charge, even if he ultimately handed off the investigation to the FBI.

Leaving Daisy to keep an eye on the five partygoers who had stumbled out of the forest, he went to the boot hill to wrangle the crew of law enforcement personnel. His assignment for the state patrolman was to take fingerprints from the victim and run her photo through facial recognition software to get a solid identification. The deputies were given forensic tasks, and he sent the rangers back to the campground to take statements before the partygoers dispersed. Daisy would stay with him to record his interviews with Pinkie and her friends. *Unprofessional? Yeah, probably.* He shouldn't use a civilian for investigative business, but he needed to talk to these people before they had time to put their heads together and make sure their stories matched. One of them might slip up and say something useful. One of them could be the killer.

Their spokeswoman was Pinkie. The death of her friend had sobered her up, and she gave cogent answers to his questions. The woman with the butterfly tattoo was Rene Williams, twenty-three years old and a part-time student at the University of Colorado campus in Denver, as were most of the attendees at the party. Rene had gone missing the night before last, but nobody worried about her absence. She'd come on this camping trip to escape her depression after breaking up with her boyfriend. "I thought she wanted to be alone," Pinkie said. "That was why she left."

"Do you have a phone number and address for the boyfriend?" Carter asked.

"I don't. He and Rene lived together, but he moved out a week ago. I never knew his phone number. Do you think he..." She sucked down a breath of mountain air and forced herself to continue. "Did he kill her?"

"Too early to speculate. How long have you been camping?"

"The original group, including Rene, has been here for four days. We're all going back to Denver tomorrow."

The conditions for these interviews couldn't have been much worse. All five of these people were functioning at varying levels of intoxication. They could overhear each other. And he only had a small recorder and spiral notebook to keep track of what they said. *Definitely not ideal.*

He considered backing off, waiting for the FBI agents to swoop in and take over. The evidence he uncovered would be checked and rechecked anyway. He felt a light squeeze on his arm and gazed down at Daisy. The spark of intelligence in her light green eyes encouraged him more than a pep talk. She didn't need to say out loud that she believed in him. Her attitude radiated confidence. He suspected that she was a hell of a good teacher.

"The guy with the buzz cut," she said, "might be one of the last people to see Rene alive. His name is Slade Franklin."

He grinned, glad that he had this smart, lovely civilian for backup. "You're paying attention."

"I remember what you said about finding the killer before he attacked anyone else. It's up to you, Carter, to protect the people in this forest."

A big job, and he might not be up to the challenge. But she was right. He had to try. Turning toward the others, he waved the big guy over. "Slade Franklin, join us."

After Daisy read back her notes and repeated his name and address in Pueblo, Slade took a seat on a sawed-off tree stump that stood taller than the sagebrush. Carter remained standing for this interrogation. "Tell me about the last time you saw Rene."

"She wasn't hanging around with the others. She looked lonely, and I felt bad for her. So I went over and talked to her."

"You didn't know her before you came to the party."

"No, sir."

"What did you talk about?"

"Her dumbass ex-boyfriend. I never met the guy, but I can tell you right now that he didn't deserve Rene. There was something about her that made me think I'd met her before."

"But you hadn't."

"No."

Carter asked, "Did you think she might go out with you?"

"I guess so. She didn't have any problem going skinny-dipping."

"Both naked?"

"Naw, she wore her underpants and bra. We went to my camper truck to change afterward. She was real pretty." He gave a sheepish grin. "I knew it was a bad idea to date a woman who was getting over a breakup, but I didn't care."

"Did you try to kiss her?" Carter considered the possibility of Slade making an unwanted advance on Rene. "Maybe you rubbed her back while she was changing clothes."

"She didn't want me to get close, and I had to

back off. My mama taught me to be polite." In spite of his size and his buzz cut, Slade seemed to be a sensitive guy. "I know what it feels like to get dumped. It's miserable."

"Then what happened with Rene?"

"We left the campground and went to a nearby lake. It's called Teacup on account of its small and almost perfectly round. She gave me some good advice about my relationship with my ex. And then her boyfriend showed up."

Carter checked his notes. "Josh Santana?"

"Yeah, it was Josh. He grabbed her and started kissing her, and she seemed to like it, even though she told me he was a jerk."

"That must have made you mad."

"It sure did."

Carter's sat phone buzzed. Caller ID showed a name he didn't recognize. "Excuse me, I need to get this."

The call came from the Pueblo-based FBI agents assigned to the investigation. They were on the road but lost, which wasn't a big surprise. The locals could easily find the ghost town, but Butcher's Gulch wasn't on regular maps. He told the agents to track the campground on their GPS, and the rangers who were there could give them directions.

When he returned, he found Daisy asking questions. "Are you a student, Slade?"

"No, ma'am. I'm thirty-one, and I work as a carpenter."

"How did you hear about the party?"

"I didn't," he said. "I came up here in my truck camper to get away from the heat in Pueblo. It's only June, but it's hotter than August. The mountains are always ten degrees cooler."

"By yourself?" she asked with just enough edge to suggest there might be something strange about a solo trip.

"Nothing wrong with that." Taken aback, he scowled at her. "You came here alone, didn't you? Somebody might think it was strange for you to be hanging around in a graveyard."

"I couldn't leave."

"Why not?"

"Because, Mr. Franklin, I found the body."

Until she allowed him to turn the focus back on her, she'd been doing a good job, even though she wasn't a trained investigator. Carter stepped in to derail this line of questioning. "Sorry for the interruption."

"No problem."

"Let's go back to what happened at the lake, Slade." Carter used the other man's first name to emphasize that the ranger was the person in authority. "After Josh arrived, did you go back to the campsite?"

"I didn't feel like socializing. I went to my camper and hit the sack." He exhaled a heavy sigh. "Maybe I sat outside for a while and watched for Rene. But I never saw her, never again."

Flashing lights and a siren from the direction of the many vehicles in the ghost town announced the arrival of an ambulance. Though these victims had no need for paramedics, the ambulance might be needed to transport the bodies to a place designated by the FBI for autopsies. They still had to wait for the coroner and/or medical examiner.

Carter kept juggling as fast as he could, but his interviews with the other three people were rushed. Over objections from Pinkie and Slade who wanted to stay close to the action, he sent them back to the campground and told them to report to the rangers on-site.

He motioned to Daisy. Together, they returned to Butcher's Gulch, where the paramedics stood beside Deputy Escobar's vehicle. They were staring at him, challenging him with their gazes. Again, he felt the pressure of being in charge, figuring out who should do what.

Daisy said, "I'd like to help."

She didn't belong here. A high school biology teacher and part-time treasure hunter had no business taking part in a murder investigation, but he wanted her to stay, wanted to hear her opinion after the dust settled. He seized on the only excuse he could think of. "You can't leave until the FBI takes your statement. After that, I'll arrange for a ride to Leadville."

"I'd rather wait until you can take me."

He was exceedingly glad to hear it. "It could be late."

"Don't care." She shrugged. "I have a vested interest, after all. You promised I could watch an autopsy."

"Fine with me." More than fine, actually. Though practically a stranger, she seemed like the only friendly face in this crowd. He handed her his car keys. "If you want to get away from the chaos, feel free to hide out in my car."

When another SUV joined the others, the ghost town began to resemble a backwoods parking lot. Unlike the other vehicles, this black Chevy Tahoe had no special logo. It dodged around the ambulance, the state police car, the deputy's SUV, the two from the National Park Service and Jackknife's beat-up truck. When they parked, two men emerged. Both wore black vests with *FBI* stenciled on the back. Without waiting to consult with anybody else, they stormed down the hill toward the body. The feds were here to take control and catch the killer.

DAISY AVOIDED THE FBI and the paramedics, making a beeline for Deputy Escobar, who still leaned against the fender of his SUV. Apparently, his task was to direct all these people to the various sites, and he didn't seem to mind playing the role of traffic cop. She guessed his age was close to fifty, old enough to have developed a thick skin and a steady calm.

From the corner of her eye, she watched Carter shake hands with the special agents. One of them seemed to know him, but they weren't friendly. In the hierarchy of local law enforcement, the feds had to be the top of the food chain. Carter had readily admitted that they had the best experts and equipment.

Standing beside Escobar, she had a sweeping view of the boot hill and noticed that the second body site was also illuminated by the portable spotlights. She glanced at the man beside her. "I bet you've seen this before."

"Whenever there's a major crime, everybody comes sniffing around. Hail, hail, the gang's all here."

"Have you ever investigated a serial killer before?"

"Never have." He folded his arms across his chest. "And I've never heard of a killer who left his victims in a graveyard. You know there was another one, didn't you?"

She nodded. "Two women."

"Three bodies," he said. "There was another in Glenwood Springs. Three of them. That's why the murderer counts as a serial killer."

"I think Carter might have mentioned it. But he didn't give me details."

"Do you want to hear?"

She bobbed her head. "But first, I remember that you mentioned sandwiches."

"There's a cooler in the back seat. Help yourself."

Escobar was, by far, her favorite among all the investigators…except for Carter, of course. She stuck her head into the back, found the heavy-duty thermal cooler, unzipped the top and peeked inside. Escobar's wife had packed six meat-and-cheese sandwiches with sliced tomatoes and lettuce in plastic bags to the side.

She called out to him. "Do you want anything?"

"I'm sticking to coffee. Help yourself to bottled water."

As she added the tomatoes and lettuce to her basic sandwich, Daisy realized that she hadn't eaten since lunch. She hadn't planned to spend so much time being lost with Jackknife, finding bodies and recording information from suspects. Nor had she expected to run into someone like Ranger A. P. Carter, who made her want to stay even later and spend time with him.

She returned to stand beside Escobar. "Thanks so much. I'm hungry."

"Even after looking at dead bodies?"

"Yup."

"You're a strange one," he said. "I wish my kids had a teacher like you. Somebody who makes learning fun."

"I love my job." She chomped into the sandwich. Hadn't Carter said something exactly like that about liking what he did for a living? They had so much in common. Too bad he lived in the mountains and she in town. Daisy wasn't a fan of long-distance relationships.

"The first victim," Escobar said, "was found about ten days ago in the Linwood Cemetery in Glenwood Springs. I saw it in police reports. She was lying in the dirt outside the wrought iron fence around the marker for Doc Holliday."

"Have you been to the grave?"

"Took the kids. My wife said it was educational. The legend on the marker says, 'Died in Bed.' A disappointment to Doc, because he wanted to die in action."

The ongoing commotion in the Butcher's Gulch boot hill and the many different law enforcement entities made her wonder about jurisdiction in that first murder. "Why was Carter involved? I thought crimes committed in cemeteries were investigated by the city."

"Glenwood Springs PD," he said with a nod. "The Park Service was called to consult because of the unusual layout of Linwood Cemetery. To reach the memorial for Doc Holliday, you have to hike almost a mile through a forest."

"Like Buffalo Bill Cody," she said. "Do you know about him? He's buried on top of Lookout Mountain outside Denver."

"Doc Holliday wasn't much like Cody. Buffalo

Bill was a showman. Doc was a gunslinger, famous for the part he played in the shootout at the OK Corral and flat broke when he died. His part of the cemetery was a potter's field for poor folks."

"Sad." She sighed. "Doc Holliday didn't get really famous until the movies."

Escobar chuckled under his breath. "Remember that line from *Tombstone*? About being someone's huckleberry. In the movie, Doc says that to Wyatt."

Meaning Doc would follow his friend anywhere like Tom Sawyer and Huckleberry Finn. She wondered if that sentiment might apply to her and Carter. Hopefully not. She wanted to be more than a pal. She wanted to press herself into his embrace and feel his lips against hers. Pushing those thoughts aside, she said, "We've gotten off topic."

"Not much else to say about the victim in Glenwood. Her name was Hannah Guerrero, and she was a dental assistant."

"Wasn't Doc Holliday a dentist?"

"Irony."

She noticed that yet another vehicle had parked at the end of the line of cars winding through Butcher's Gulch. An older man carrying an old-fashioned doctor's bag ambled toward them. Escobar introduced her to the county coroner, a retired general practitioner with a thick white mustache. The coroner nodded to the deputy and asked what was going on.

Graciously, the deputy deferred to her. "Ms.

Brighton discovered the first body. She's a biology teacher and can give you details on the medical stuff."

"I can sum it up in one word—dead." She appreciated the gesture from Escobar but didn't want to mislead this former doctor. "Is there anything specific you want to know?"

"I doubt I'll have enough accurate information for the death certificate. The ME will have to fill in the blanks." He shrugged. "Can you tell me how these women died?"

"Homicide," she said. "There were bloody wounds at the throat, but I can't say for sure that cause of death was exsanguination."

His bushy eyebrows lifted, and she saw respect dawning. "What about time of death?"

She ran through her observations on body temp, onset of rigor, bloating, skin discoloration and the presence of blowfly eggs and maggots. "But I agree with you. The actual TOD is better left to the medical examiner."

One of the paramedics joined their group. "You need to sign off on the bodies so we can figure out whether or not we need to transport them."

"Well, that's going to depend on who's in charge—the county sheriff's deputies, the Colorado state patrol, FBI or NPS."

With the investigation spinning in so many different directions, she couldn't imagine how Carter was going to proceed. After she thanked Escobar for the sandwich, Daisy made her way through the array of vehicles to Carter's SUV. Jackknife's truck was parked directly behind him, and the old man yelled at her as she came close. She blocked out his words. He was not her problem.

Glad that Carter had the foresight to give her access to his car, she opened the door using his key fob, slipped into the rear and stretched out across three seats. Though the night wasn't cold, she was glad to find a plaid wool blanket and a pillow. If Carter had attempted to sleep back here, he would have been totally uncomfortable. Though she was slightly taller than average, she fit nicely.

Before she fell asleep, her imagination conjured up an image of herself lying beside Carter with his arms encircling her. She was ready for sweet dreams.

Chapter Five

Daisy jolted awake when the car parked. The engine continued to hum, and she heard triumphant instrumental music from the CD player. *A soundtrack? For what?* Her eyelids blinked open, and she remembered climbing into the back seat of Carter's SUV. Sitting up, she held the plaid wool blanket in front of her to block the chill. Outside the windows, she saw a wall of trees.

She shook off the vestiges of sleep, stretched her spine and rotated her shoulders. Daisy had always been a morning person, quickly alert. "Where are we?"

"Not too far from Butcher's Gulch," Carter said as he twisted around in his seat to look at her. "It's after five thirty, the edge of dawn."

"So early."

"Or late," he said, "depending on your point of view."

Last night when she curled up in here, it had been before midnight. She'd slept for over five hours—must have been more tired than she realized. She inhaled a deep breath and listened to the classical music as Carter hummed along to the music from *Star Wars* by John Williams. "May the force be with you."

"I like to think it is."

Up till now, he'd kept the geekier side of his personality hidden, like his smile. But Carter was almost as nerdy as any of her high school students. "Do you think of yourself as Obi-Wan? Or Luke Skywalker?"

"Neither."

"Of course not." She groaned. "Han Solo."

"You've got to love him." He turned off the music and opened his door. "Come with me."

She didn't have time to ask where they were going. Before she had her feet planted on the ground, he was already halfway down a gradual slope. The early-morning breeze brushed against her cheeks—fresh, bracing and pine scented. With the sunrise blushing a delicate pink in the sky, flashlights weren't necessary, but she picked her way carefully until she emerged from the forest.

Standing on the rocky shore of a small lake, she watched the pastel dawn reflect on the sparkling waters and shimmer in the spiky treetops. Without saying a word, Carter stood close beside her and took her hand. Though they'd only met last night and nothing had happened between them, they shared an intimacy.

"Teacup Lake." He pointed across the crystalline waters to the north. "That's where Josh found Rene and Slade."

Her hand felt safe and warm in his unexpectedly familiar grasp. "Did you have a chance to talk to the witnesses again?"

"I did a quick interview of your buddy, Jackknife Jones. He admitted that he purposely got lost when he was driving. Somebody paid him to not take you to Butcher's Gulch until after dark."

"That's ominous. Did he say who?"

"Didn't know the guy, and I'm not sure he was telling the truth. Jackknife might have wanted to get you alone after dark."

She shuddered. "What about the others?"

"According to the one you call Pinkie, Rene used to bathe in the lake."

"Naked?"

"That's usually the way you take a bath," he said. "I talked to others at the campsite. One of the guys claimed he knew you. His name is Eric Wolff."

Irritation shot through her, and she tensed, inadvertently squeezing Carter's hand. "The Wolff family—Eric and his father, Gerald—are direct descendants of Morris Wolff, who was part of Sherwood Brighton's outlaw gang. Eric has exaggerated the role of his ancestor to partner and claims to have information that will lead to the bullion, which he thinks is half his."

"None of the others at the party recognized him as part of their regular gang."

"Like Slade Franklin," she pointed out.

"And there were a couple of other young men who were drawn to the music, free beer and women in cutoff jeans." He paused to look down at her. The first rays of the sun glowed on his cheekbones and sculpted chin. "Do you think Eric was looking for you?"

"Yes." Her gaze lowered to his lips, and she imagined what their kiss would be like—their first kiss. She looked away from him before she did something she might regret. "It can't be a coincidence that he was there."

"What else do you know about this guy?" Carter asked.

"Like my aunt, he believes the key to finding the treasure is locating Sherwood Brighton's grave." She blamed Eric and his father for her quest to locate grave sites. "His reasoning comes from letters written to Morris Wolff. I think there were a couple from Annie Brighton, Sherwood's wife. Anyway, Aunt Vi believes he's onto something."

"Did he ever mention Glenwood or Doc Holliday?"

"I don't think so." She frowned. "You're thinking of the first victim."

"Hannah Guerrero," he said.

"Was she posed in the same position as Rene and the other woman?"

"There were similarities." He turned his head to stare across the rippling waves. "Flat on her back, fully dressed with hands folded on her stomach. A long silk scarf was tied around her throat. Apparently, she'd been killed where she lay. Her blood spread across the dirt and got in her long black hair."

"Black hair?"

"She didn't resemble either of the other victims," he said. "The killer doesn't have a type."

"Was Hannah from Glenwood?"

"It was a nearby town, like Carbondale or Basalt. Her friends described her as sociable, easygoing and gullible—the kind of person who believed every crazy story, which makes me think she would have loved your treasure hunt. I wish I could have done more to find her killer."

"What did the police ask you to do?"

"To see if I could learn anything from the trail that led up to the memorial. A well-traveled path with too many footprints. Long story short—I didn't find much. No signs of a struggle. There was an imprint in the dirt of Hannah's shoes and a pair of size-thirteen sneakers."

"A big man?"

"Not necessarily," he said. "The important thing is that each of his footprints were outside hers and facing the same direction."

"How does that work?"

When she tried to move into the position the footprints indicated, he spun her around until she stood in front of him with her shoulders against his chest. "Like this," he said.

"Why?"

In answer, he slung an arm around her middle to hold her in place. With the opposite hand, he drew an imaginary blade across her throat. His action took only a few seconds. "That's one way it could have happened."

"He would have gotten blood all over his clothes."

"Unless he released her immediately." Suiting the action to the word, he dropped his arms and stepped back. "He severed the carotid. She might have staggered a few paces before she lost consciousness and fell to the ground. The blood spatters indicate that sort of scenario."

"Gruesome." Talking about the murder disturbed her a lot more than analyzing the bodily remains. She'd also been thrown off balance by their sudden physical contact. Even when he was illustrating a murder scene, Carter's nearness felt good to her.

He continued, "I also found that the killer wiped his shoes on the pine needles before he hiked down. It looked like he and Hannah walked up there together."

"Which meant he was someone she trusted."

"Or wasn't afraid to be alone with after dark."

The gap between trusting someone and not being afraid of them spread as wide as a chasm. In all the years she'd been dating, Daisy was notoriously slow to trust. Only once had she allowed a relationship to develop into living together, an arrangement that lasted only eight months. On the other hand, she was seldom afraid of being alone with a person she'd just met. Hadn't she hopped into Jackknife's truck without giving him a second thought?

She asked, "Is it possible that the killer was her boyfriend?"

"I don't remember all the details. It wasn't my case," he said. "All I've got are the basics. On the night of her murder, Hannah and her friends were at a tavern in Glenwood. She left at ten o'clock to meet a guy who was an Old West fanatic and curious about Doc Holliday's ghost."

"Sounds like Eric Wolff," she said. "I'm also pretty sure that he was the person who paid Jackknife to make sure I got to the boot hill after dark."

"One of her friends said Hannah had the feeling that she was being stalked."

"Again," Daisy said, "that's something Eric would do."

"This friend got worried when she couldn't reach Hannah on her cell phone. She went searching and found the body."

Daisy wondered if Carter would interview this friend. If he was in charge of the investigation, he'd surely start there, contacting the Glenwood PD. "Who will you be working with on that investigation?"

"The FBI has jurisdiction on serial killers." He continued to gaze across the waters as the forest came to life with the twittering of sparrows and buntings. A speckled owl swooped across the lake, ending his nocturnal hunt and disappearing into the forest. "The feds can use their cyberexperts to search for similar murders in different states and locations. And they'll do background checks on all the suspects."

"Including Jackknife?"

"He's a suspect. I'm not taking him off my list, but he isn't in the number one slot. These murders were probably the work of a younger, stronger man."

"Why do you think so?" she asked.

"I'm guessing he was boyfriend material, good-looking enough to entice Hannah into leaving her friends at the bar. And Rene Williams, the barefoot woman you found, was probably killed elsewhere and carried to her final resting place in the boot hill. She was a small woman, but it still takes muscles to carry a dead weight."

"You're good at this." She met his steady gaze. "Are you okay with not being in charge?"

"I don't miss tangling with all those different branches of law enforcement. If I'm not the boss, I have more freedom and fewer rules." He glided the back of his hand down her cheek and tilted her chin up toward him. "And I don't have to worry about confiding in a smart, pretty civilian like you."

He thinks I'm pretty. "I wouldn't want you to get in trouble."

"You're no trouble at all."

He dipped his head and kissed her lightly. The gentle pressure started a ripple of sensation that grew more intense when she arched her back and fitted her body against him. Her lungs squeezed, and she could barely catch her breath.

As their kiss continued and deepened, she melted. Her legs turned to jelly. For a moment, she thought she'd swoon like a naive ingenue in a melodrama, but Daisy wasn't a weak-kneed damsel. Strength counted as one of her best assets. Determinedly, she stepped away from his embrace and stared at him, wide-eyed and aroused with her heart wildly palpitating. *Say something.* Her lower lip trembled. "The autopsy," she blurted. "Can I still watch the autopsy?"

"I'll do my best to arrange it."

"When?"

"Probably later today. In the afternoon."

She clung to the solid thought of seeing the autopsy as though it was a life raft in a sea of confusion. He'd have to take her to the medical examiner, which meant they'd be together, and she'd have another chance to be calm, cool and collected. "What do we do next?"

"I take you home to your aunt Vi."

She caught her breath as she climbed the hill behind him. *Inhale...exhale...inhale.* Her aunt was going to adore Carter. Since Daisy's retired parents had moved to Australia, Vi had donned the mantle of parenthood and never missed a chance to nag about how Daisy should settle down and get married. Vi would see the handsome ranger as an excellent candidate for Mr. Right.

WHILE THEY DROVE, Carter filled her in on the direction of the investigation. "This afternoon, we need to hook up with the FBI in Pueblo so you can give your statement. I've worked with one of the agents before. His name is Pat Wiley, and he's a straight shooter."

"There were two of them last night."

"The other is Mickey Hicks."

"Sounds like a cartoon character."

"That's a fairly accurate description, but he's not a mouse. He looks like Popeye."

Carter felt his eyelids drooping. He hadn't slept much last night and needed a burst of caffeine to jump-start his brain. He wasn't thinking right, which might explain why he'd kissed Daisy. Not a rational decision—he'd acted on impulse without considering the consequences. A mistake? Or the smartest move he'd ever made?

He pulled off and parked at a diner he knew had decent coffee. The food wasn't great, but he needed calories for energy. Daisy, an early bird, chowed down and chatted while downing her own coffee. Watching her gave him more vigor than the caffeine. Fairly quickly, they got back on the road.

At a few minutes after nine o'clock, they arrived at Aunt Vi's two-story, gingerbread Victorian house in the historic district of Leadville. The color scheme of gray, black and lilac qualified this place as a "painted lady" without being too showy—a description that might also apply to the woman who posed on the wide veranda and watched him park in the driveway. Like Daisy, Aunt Violet had streaked blond hair. Unlike Daisy, who usually wore her hair in a tumbledown ponytail, Vi's hair was cut to chin length, straight with bangs. Though Daisy had told him that her aunt was sixty-eight, she could have passed for ten or even twenty years younger.

When Daisy came around the SUV and stood beside him, he said, "Your aunt looks like she belongs in that painted-lady house."

"She's perfected a style that I call classic Western. A tailored shirt tucked into a midcalf, faux-leather skirt and snakeskin cowboy boots. The jewelry is, of course, silver and turquoise." She gave her aunt a good-natured grin and waved. "On some people the outfit would be cliché, but Vi pulls it off."

When Daisy introduced him, Violet gave him a handshake and a perfect smile with precisely applied dark red lipstick. "Should I be worried, Ranger Carter, about my niece not coming home last night?"

"I apologize, ma'am. We got caught up in a serial killer investigation."

Her eyebrows lifted, but she maintained her composure. "Won't you come inside? I should mention that I have another guest. You've met him before, Daisy. Eric Wolff."

Carter scanned the curb in front of the house. His gaze stuck on a dark blue van with the logo for Wolff House Painting and a pyramid of gallon paint cans on the side. Beside him, Daisy growled. "He's not our friend. Eric showed up last night near the murder scene, which makes me think he might have been following me. As a matter of fact, I'm going to ask him right now."

She charged through the front door, leaving him and her aunt on the front porch. If Carter had been in charge of the investigation, he would have reined Daisy in before she physically assaulted a suspect, but he had neither the authority nor the inclination to stop her. Her anger might push Eric into saying something incriminating.

He held the door for Vi. "After you, ma'am."

"I hope you won't mind if I ask a personal question," she said. "Are you married?"

"Not married. Not engaged."

Her red-lipstick smile widened like a Cheshire cat. "Would you like coffee? And a homemade cinnamon scone?"

"Yes, please."

While Vi strode down the central hallway toward what he assumed was the kitchen, he followed the sound of Daisy's voice into a sitting room that was furnished with an eclectic combination of ornate antiques and furniture of many styles and eras. He didn't know much about interior decorating, but he liked this room. It showed personality.

Daisy had positioned herself in front of Eric Wolff, who slouched in a burgundy velvet wing-back chair beside a chrome end table. Her voice hit a stern, authoritative note, reminding him that she was a high school teacher who regularly dealt with cranky adolescents. The age didn't apply to Wolff, who was in his thirties, but the attitude was a fit.

"I'll ask you again," Daisy said, "did you follow me to that campground?"

"You aren't the center of the world, Daisy."

"I think you've been stalking me." She glanced over at Carter. "That's illegal, isn't it?"

"You could file a restraining order compelling Mr. Wolff to stay away from you."

Eric curled his arms tightly against his body. "I didn't do anything wrong."

His shoulder-length blond hair fell around his boyish face in limp, tangled strands. Though he wasn't fat, his cheeks were pudgy, and he had a button nose. From the interview at the campground, Carter knew Eric's age, address in Pueblo and occupation—if he could call being an unemployed housepainter a real job.

"Nice van," Carter said. "Do you take jobs in places other than Pueblo?"

"Sure." His shoulders hunched.

"Ever worked in Glenwood Springs?"

"Yeah. Why?"

"Around the tenth of June, were you in Glenwood?"

His gaze shifted nervously. "I'd have to check my schedule."

Vi entered the room carrying a tray with coffee mugs for Daisy and Carter along with sugar and cream. She placed the tray on a large marble-topped coffee table, and the fresh-roasted aroma wafted pleasantly through the room. Vi straightened. "Daisy, please come to the kitchen with me. I need help carrying the scones."

Carter sat on the long sofa nearest Eric's chair, took off his cowboy hat and picked up his coffee mug. He didn't use cream or sugar, especially not on good, strong coffee like this with subtle undertones of nuts and berries. A far cry from the diner.

He licked his lips and glanced over at Eric. Several possible questions rattled around in Carter's head, but he wasn't sure where to start. The silent treatment had proved effective for him in past interviews. Eric seemed immature and nervous—the sort of man who needed to start talking to fill an uncomfortable silence. He'd say too much rather than too little.

Daisy didn't like him, which was reason enough for Carter to suspect this thirtysomething guy who lived with his father in Pueblo. What was the deal with Eric Wolff? Was he a stalker, too afraid to approach Daisy directly? Or was he a killer?

"Do I need to get a lawyer?" Eric asked.

“Have you done something illegal?”

“Hell, no,” he said. “Daisy is the one you ought to be investigating. She has all kinds of secrets. She and Vi are cheating me and my dad out of millions.”

Daisy stalked into the room, carrying another tray with napkins, silverware, clotted cream and two flavors of jam. “You’re a liar.”

Aunt Vi followed with the scones on a separate plate. “Settle down. Both of you.”

Carter wanted to pounce on the cinnamon scones and not listen to their bickering. His cell phone bleeped, indicating a text message coming through, and he grabbed the excuse. “Excuse me, I need to take this.” Caller ID showed it was from the FBI.

He went to the front door, opened the screen and stepped onto the porch before tapping on the text. Agent Wiley had identified the blonde he’d found at the boot hill using fingerprints. Her name was Andrea Lindstrom. Why did that sound so familiar? Who was she? The gang partying at the campground hadn’t mentioned her.

Carter studied the accompanying photo from her driver’s license, and the puzzle pieces clicked into place. He knew her.

He looked away from the image on the screen. Last night, he’d stared down at her ravaged remains in the shallow grave. Half her face had been torn away. The silk scarf at her throat had been encrusted with blood. In his mind, he erased that horrific image. Instead, he remembered a day when he'd talked to this sweet, gentle woman about the tragic death of her dear friend Hannah Guerrero.

Andrea had been reported missing on the fourteenth.

Was that timing correct? Hannah was killed on June 10, and Andrea disappeared on June 14. But Daisy had placed time of death for Andrea at two or three days ago, which would have been June 17. Where had she been between the time when she went missing and when she died?

Chapter Six

Still wondering about the link between two of the victims, Carter put away his phone, opened the screen door and stepped back into the house. Standing outside the sitting room, he paused to listen before entering. He didn't hear Daisy yelling or Eric whimpering, which was a good sign, because he didn't want to spend the day on a childish spitting match. Aunt Vi was lecturing them both on the standards of courteous behavior that separated civilized beings from the beasts.

After an apology for slipping out, Carter returned to his seat and broke off a piece of scone, which he slathered with clotted cream and strawberry jam. Daisy sat at the opposite end of the sofa, as far away from Eric as she could get. Her cheeks were flushed with an angry red, her jaw thrust out at a stubborn angle and the line of her soft, sensuous lips had flattened. If Eric was angry, he didn't show it. His shoulders had caved in on his baggy midsection. His mouth trembled, and his watery blue eyes flickered on the verge of tears.

"Thank you, Miss Violet," Eric said, sounding like a child. "I never ever meant to insult you. Or Daisy."

An indecipherable rumble came from Daisy.

Vi gave her a harsh glance. "Did you have something to say, dear? Speak up."

Carter filled his mouth with scone to keep from laughing at Daisy's obvious struggle to control her outrage.

"I'm sorry for raising my voice," Daisy said. "I have a simple question for our guest."

"Go ahead and ask," Aunt Vi said, playing mediator.

"Eric, did you follow me to the campground?"

"No," he said quickly. "You didn't see me following, did you?"

Carter sipped coffee to wash down the scone. He believed Eric. Not because he was innocent, but there were other ways to keep track of another person's whereabouts. Also, he didn't think Eric was capable of following without being noticed. He wasn't a hunter.

"A follow-up," Daisy said. "Did you pay Jackknife to stall until after dark before bringing me to the boot hill?"

He looked down and shrugged. "Not really."

Carter didn't believe him.

"Another question," he said. "Where were you this morning before you came to Leadville?"

"Sleeping. Why?"

"Did you sleep in your van instead of driving all the way home to Pueblo?"

Eric gave a nod. "Nothing wrong with that."

"Think back to dawn." Carter lowered his voice

to a soothing, nonthreatening level. "One of the prettiest times of the day, when the skies turn pink and the soft light reflects on the surface of the water. Don't you think so?"

"Yes," he said hesitantly.

"Birds chirping. Waves rippling," Carter said. "So beautiful."

"Yeah."

"Tell me, Eric. Were you at Teacup Lake this morning?"

"Maybe I was." As soon as the words slipped out, he clapped his hand over his mouth as if he could stuff his confession back inside. "Okay, I saw you there. Saw what you were doing."

"You're keeping an eye on Daisy," Carter said. "How are you doing it? A tracking device in her pocket? A locator hooked up to her phone?"

"Who was doing what to whom?" Vi asked.

"You're worse than a stalker." Daisy's lip curled in a snarl. "You've been spying on me."

"Listen, Daisy, all I want is for us to work together. I really need to find the treasure. Me and my dad have a bunch of debt. If we don't get some kind of payoff, we'll lose the house. I'll never have the kind of future I deserve."

"What do you think you deserve?" Carter asked.

"A home with a sweet wife and two kids, girl and boy. And a golden retriever like I had before my mother left us. She took the dog with her. What kind of woman does that?"

He sounded far more upset about losing his pet puppy than having his mother desert the family. In some ways, he seemed normal—pathetic, but normal. In others, he behaved like a creepy stalker.

"Why would I help you?" Daisy asked.

"I have information about the Brighton Bullion that would help your search, and I'll bet there are plenty of things you can tell me."

"Prove it," Daisy said. "Show me one of those letters to Morris Wolff that you're always bragging about. You said you had several from Sherwood Brighton's wife."

He dug into an inner pocket of his lightweight canvas jacket. "When we find the treasure, we split it right down the middle. Fifty-fifty."

"You get twenty percent," she countered.

"Forty."

"Twenty-five," she said. "Final offer."

He stood and held a folded sheet of paper just out of her grasp. For the first time, Carter realized that Eric might look soft and dumpy, but, under that layer of fat, he was actually above average height and in decent physical condition.

With a cold laugh, he handed her the paper. "It's a copy. When you're done reading it, call me and give me an equally important clue."

With his pug nose in the air, he stomped across the patterned Oriental rug and exited from the house. Daisy bolted to her feet and chased after him. “Wait up,” she said. “I want to know how you’re tracking me. Did you bug my phone?”

Carter followed her. He couldn’t compel Eric to hand over his tracking devices, a fact that he considered a gigantic lapse in the legal system, but he wanted the jerk to realize that he was creating a problem for himself. Standing at the screen door, Carter said, “I’d advise you to cooperate.”

“Fine.” Eric’s lower lip stuck out. “There’s a tracker in the change compartment of your wallet.”

“How did you put it there?”

“Let’s just say that you should watch your purse more carefully. Anyway, you can take it out and pitch it. I won’t be able to follow you on my GPS.”

Daisy gave him a reluctant nod. “You better not be lying.”

“And you better call me. We’ve got a deal.”

When Carter turned back toward the sitting room, Aunt Vi stood in his way. Her small fists were planted on her hips below her Navajo concha belt. In a stern voice, she asked, “What was Eric saying about what he saw at the lake?”

“Eric was spying,” he said, hoping to distract her. “It doesn’t seem right that those tracking devices you can order online are legal. There ought to be a law against following a person without their permission. If he was a Peeping Tom, I could arrest him.”

“I once had a peeper,” she said in a whisper. “It

was right after I divorced my second husband, and I wasn't accustomed to taking care of myself."

Mission accomplished: he'd diverted her from talking about the kiss. "What did you do?"

"Well, I bought a gun." A sly smile teased the corners of her lips. "The first of many. Thanks to the peeper, I discovered how much I enjoy shooting things."

Carter would definitely keep that in mind. His phone buzzed with another text message from Special Agent Pat Wiley. Both of the boot hill victims had been dosed with knockout drugs. Rene Williams also had a blood alcohol level of 0.13, indicating that she'd continued drinking after she left the party at the campground.

When Daisy came back toward the porch, where he and Vi were standing, she had her wallet in hand and had pulled out the small tracking device, which she threw down on the sidewalk and stomped on. "That's what I think of Eric Wolff."

"Are you sure you destroyed it?" Vi asked. "Should I get my gun?"

Carter couldn't tell if she was joking and decided not to hang around and find out. As he left the veranda, he spoke to Daisy. "I need to make a few phone calls, but I'll be back in an hour or so and we'll drive down to the FBI office in Pueblo so you can give your statement."

"I'll be ready and waiting."

As he strode toward his SUV, he heard Aunt Vi

return to the prior topic. "This is the last time I'm going to ask, Daisy. What happened at the lake?"

At the curb, Carter ducked into his car and took off. He wasn't sure where he was headed but knew he needed some space. Any other location was preferable to a relationship discussion with the well-armed Aunt Violet.

MUCH AS DAISY wanted to avoid the topic of her kiss with Carter at the edge of Teacup Lake, she knew Aunt Vi wouldn't give up until she got an answer. "If I tell you, will you drop the subject?"

"Probably not. I need to stay informed about the doings of my niece. Leadville isn't like the big city. People here watch out for each other. And they gossip. Lord, how they gossip!"

Daisy wasn't sure how her behavior reflected on her aunt. After all, she was supposed to be a wicked woman from the big city, and they expected her to have loose morals. Her actions weren't Vi's fault. "Carter and I were kissing."

"I approve." Vi gave a brisk nod. "He seems like a nice young man with a respectable job as a forest ranger. Your summer visit might have gotten much more exciting."

"Just a kiss. It doesn't mean anything."

"But it could." Vi gave her a friendly little pat on the bottom like a coach sending a new player into the game. "Run along, dear. He's going to be picking you up again in a little while, and you should get ready. Take a shower, wash your hair and put on some makeup."

Muttering under her breath, Daisy climbed the staircase, crossed the landing and went into her bedroom on the second floor. She'd intended to get cleaned up and change clothes. Not to look more seductive but because she expected this day to be long and possibly complicated. After the FBI interview, she hoped to be attending the autopsy, which wasn't an occasion for getting all dolled up, but she wanted to look clean and sanitary.

Uninvited, Aunt Vi stepped into her room. "Maybe you should borrow something attractive. I have a closet full of outfits I've barely worn."

"Believe me, Vi, if I was planning to make a move on Carter—or any other man, for that matter—you'd be the first person I'd consult." Her aunt was something of an expert, having gone through four husbands and innumerable boyfriends. "But there's no way I can have a serious relationship with a guy who lives in the mountains. My work is in the city, and I love my job."

"Don't be so quick to say no."

Daisy changed the topic. "I found something in Butcher's Gulch. There was a gravestone for Annie Brighton, Sherwood's wife."

"A clue," Vi said with evident delight. "Jackknife said he saw a marker for Brighton, but I wasn't sure whether I could believe him or not. He should have mentioned it was Annie."

"He wanted to impress you. Wants you to date him and fall in love because you're rich and can take care of him."

"But I'm not a wealthy woman," she protested. "And if I were, I most certainly wouldn't be interested in the likes of Jackknife Jones. I have better taste."

"I don't have a lot of information about Annie. Can you give me the highlights?"

"She and Sherwood had three children, and she basically raised them by herself. His career as an outlaw kept him away from home for days at a time." Vi referred to his supposed "career" as though he'd been a busy stockbroker. "He provided for his family, and nobody ever asked where her money came from."

"Maybe because they were scared," Daisy said under her breath.

"You have no call to bad-mouth your ancestor. From all accounts, he was a gentleman."

Except when he was robbing banks. Her proper aunt was quick to turn a blind eye when it came to the treasure. "Go on."

"Annie worked as a seamstress and was acclaimed for making fancy wedding dresses. She lived in Cripple Creek and Pueblo for most of her life."

"But was buried in Butcher's Gulch."

"Tell me more about the headstone," Vi said eagerly. "What did it say?"

"'Annie Brighton. Wife, Friend and Lover.'"

"Aw, that's so sweet. Sherwood still thought of her as his lover." She frowned. "But it doesn't make sense. I seem to remember that he died before she did."

"Maybe one of the kids was responsible for her marker."

Daisy was curious. Why was Annie buried in a boot hill cemetery, which was the final resting place for outlaws and the indigent? She seemed to be a decent woman who made wedding gowns. Why Butcher's Gulch? Who erected her tombstone? Instead of diving into the shower and washing her hair, Daisy sat on the edge of her bed and unfolded the piece of paper Eric had given her. There might be relevant clues in this copy of a letter—dated June 6, 1889—from Annie to Morris Wolff.

Vi sat beside her, reading over her shoulder. "That's two years after the theft of Brighton's Bullion. When I think about it, I'm certain that Sherwood died in 1896, nine years after the big robbery. What was the date on Annie's tombstone?"

"There wasn't one. No date of birth or death."

"Not completely uncommon," Vi said. "Some ladies are rather particular about revealing their age, even after they're dead."

Silently, Daisy read the first few lines, which were carefully written with perfect penmanship. Then she looked up, wide-eyed and surprised.

"This is hot stuff. I guess Annie B. didn't like to waste time on foreplay."

"Those descriptions are based on references from the Bible," Vi said. "Her breasts are ripe fruit, firm and juicy. Made for his delight. Could be Song of Solomon."

Annie continued with an imaginative description of Morris Wolff's private parts, which were—supposedly—as hard as oak and hung to his knees. This letter was an 1800's version of the current trend to send naked, obscene photos via text message. Annie couldn't wait until they were "joined together from top to toe" and she could "taste every sweet bite of his quivering flesh."

"Yuck," Daisy said. "I guess we know why her gravestone mentioned that she was a lover, not necessarily with her husband."

Vi pointed to the end of the letter. "This is the only place she even mentions him."

Daisy read aloud. "'Sherwood will never know where I've put the bullion. It's mine now.'"

"Those are the words of an angry woman." Violet shuddered. "We might have been researching the wrong person. Annie seems to be in charge."

"And has possession of the gold."

Daisy had to admit that Eric Wolff had shown them a telling clue for their treasure hunt. She wondered what else he might be hiding.

Chapter Seven

With the windows down, Carter drove through Leadville, one of his favorite little towns, which was part of the territory he regularly patrolled. As he left the outskirts, the late-morning sky stretched wide and blue above him. He needed this space to clear his head. While driving to a rocky hillside he'd visited before, Carter allowed the mountains to nurture his mind and his spirit.

At an elevation over ten thousand feet, Leadville—the highest incorporated town in North America—boomed into existence during the 1889 silver rush, but the real treasure was the beauty of the surroundings. Nine fourteeners, including Mount Elbert and the aptly named Mount Massive, dominated the landscape. Carter thought these peaks, still snowcapped in the latter half of June, might have provided inspiration for the explorer who saw this mountain range at dawn when the sun had painted the snow a bright red. *Sangre de Cristo* meant "blood of Christ."

Leaving the main road, he guided his NPS vehicle to a clearing at the top of a rise with a heavy-duty picnic table and benches that had seen better days. He swung open the car door, stepped into the sunshine and inhaled the scent of resin, dust and pine cones. Though he had a desk and computer at the NPS headquarters in Salida, he considered places like this—with soul-stirring views of high peaks and abundant forests—to be his office. He'd never trade this job for a cubicle.

Wishing he'd brought a thermos of Aunt Vi's excellent coffee, he stepped onto the bench, sat on the tabletop, took off his cowboy hat and welcomed the breeze that ruffled his hair. He looked to the mountains for answers. One side of his brain popped with questions about the serial killer investigation, while the other was preoccupied with Daisy. From the moment they met, he'd liked her. He admired her smart analysis of the victims' remains. The bubbling sound of her laughter made him smile. He'd never forget the way her lips tasted when they kissed.

He stared across the foothills to the rugged mountains beyond. What the hell was he going to do? The answer came fast—first, he had to stop the serial killer.

And he needed expert advice. Using the sat phone with a strong signal, he called Joaquin Stanley. His supervisor, a former hippie, brought a unique set of skills to his work. He had degrees in forestry, environmental biology and psychology. Before joining the Park Service, he'd been a farmer, a firefighter and a therapist/counselor who specialized in the treatment of perpetrators. His analysis of the serial killer's motives would provide a solid profile.

When Joaquin answered, Carter gave him a quick rundown of the progress on the investigation, including the important fact that the FBI in Pueblo had taken over jurisdiction. "The special agent in charge is SAC Pat Wiley. I've worked with him before."

"Sounds like you've got everything covered. Why are you calling me?"

"I could use your help in profiling the killer," Carter said.

"Stop by this afternoon."

"Can't. I've got an appointment at the FBI office in Pueblo. Then I'm going to watch the autopsy."

"You?" Joaquin questioned. "You've never liked the gory part of the job."

"Yeah, well, people change."

"I'm sensing something from you. What's going on?"

"Nothing." Carter knew his supervisor well. He imagined the burly man stroking his neatly trimmed, salt-and-pepper beard, a remnant of the ZZ Top look he wore in his hippie days. "I don't know what you're talking about."

"There's definite change. You're not acting like a lonesome cowboy anymore."

"Never was a cowboy." Living in the wilderness suited him, but he hadn't grown up on a ranch and didn't ride the range. Bouncing around on a horse gave him a stiff back and an achy ass.

"You know what I mean," Joaquin said. "It's

your attitude, your independent nature. You're like Gary Cooper or Clint Eastwood—a kickass loner taming the Wild West."

That description fit a lot of rangers and mountain men. "If I'm a cowboy, what are you?"

"Lumberjack," he said proudly. "My ex-wife used to like watching me chop wood. No kidding. She said it made her horny."

Though he'd come to Joaquin for his expert opinion, Carter enjoyed their wide-ranging conversations. "As long as we're talking about women..."

"Aha!" Carter heard Joaquin slam the flat of his large hand against his desktop. "I know what's different about you. You're in love. Well, good luck to you, Ranger. It's about time."

"I'm not saying you're right, but suppose I met a strong, stubborn woman who loves her life in the city and will never move to the mountains. How do I change her mind?"

"Never start a relationship thinking you can change the other person. Either you accept her as she is or you quit your job and move into town."

"You're saying it's up to me. I'm the one who has to change."

"Not necessarily. You and your lady friend can hook up for a couple of days and then go your separate ways."

A quick affair wasn't what Carter wanted. With Daisy, something more was possible—something amazing. He'd tried marriage before, and it had lasted less than two years. He wasn't good at being half of a couple. His ex-wife called him a loner. But Daisy was independent and strong and unlike any other woman he'd met. A relationship with her would be an adventure.

His gaze lifted to the vast panorama of the Sangre de Cristos. This was his home. He never wanted to live anywhere else. If she didn't change her mind…

"Profiling." He switched gears. This phone call was, after all, about the serial killer. "Here's what I can tell you about the three victims. They were all young and pretty. All were found in graveyards but might not have been killed there. Long silk scarves were tied around the fatal wounds to their throats. Two of them—Hannah and Andrea—knew each other."

"What's different about the three victims?" Joaquin asked.

"Different physical types. Hannah had black hair, dark eyes and a muscular frame. Andrea was a willowy blonde, pale skinned, not an outdoors type. And Rene Williams, the most recent victim, had long brown hair and she was petite."

"What else?"

"Different occupations. Hannah was a dental assistant. Andrea worked for an insurance company. They both lived in the Glenwood Springs area in apartments. Didn't have roommates. Rene was a college student from Denver who had just broken up with a live-in boyfriend."

"How about the times of death? When were they killed?"

"I can't be precise until after the autopsies, but Daisy made a couple of good guesses about when the women in Butcher's Gulch were killed."

"Daisy," Joaquin said. "Is she a coroner? A medical examiner?"

"A high school biology teacher from Denver." He kept his voice level to avoid betraying his feelings for her. "She teaches anatomy and studied forensic medicine at a body farm."

"And she gave you an expert opinion?"

"That's right. Records show that Hannah was murdered on June 10. Andrea was probably killed on June 17 but went missing on the fourteenth. Rene died last night, on June 20."

"First victim on the tenth, second on the seventeenth, third on the twentieth." Joaquin exhaled with a whoosh. "I can see why you need a profile ASAP. The shorter periods between kills could be an indication that he's planning another murder very soon."

"We need to act fast."

Carter heard the scrape of a chair being pushed back from a desk. He knew Joaquin was on his feet, pacing across the black-and-sienna-patterned Navajo area rug in his office. Part of his process was moving. He said physical activity jogged his brain. "When you found the bodies, what was your first impression?"

"Hannah and Rene were arranged to look like they were asleep, but Andrea's body had been mauled by predators." He thought of Daisy's suggestion that the killer had tried to shield the body. "He might have tried to protect Andrea with some kind of covering."

"Tell me about these scarves."

Carter imagined his supervisor standing at the window of his office, looking out at the Collegiate Peaks—Mount Princeton, Mount Harvard and so on. "The scarves are similar and were put on after death. I'm thinking the killer brought them with him."

"Did you find a murder weapon?"

"No." Carter shook his head. "The autopsy will tell us about the two in Butcher's Gulch. Hannah's throat was slashed by a heavy-duty hunting knife."

"Doesn't exactly narrow it down," Joaquin complained. "Sexual assault?"

"Not on Hannah. We have to wait for the autopsy to know about the other two. My gut tells me no." He described the way Rene's hair was styled and her blouse buttoned up to the collar. "So, what should I look for? I'm hoping you can be more specific than the usual parameters for a serial killer—white male between twenty-eight and forty-five. Abusive childhood. Egocentric with lack of remorse."

"An organized killer," Joaquin said. "He planned ahead, bringing a weapon and a special scarf. It's possible that his planning extends to the selection of his victims. He might get a thrill from learning her habits, might watch her or follow her."

"A stalker."

Carter thought of Eric Wolff and the tracking device he'd planted on Daisy. Though it seemed coincidental that Eric's interest in treasure hunting meshed with serial murders, he might be clever enough to hide one by focusing on the other. It ought to be easy enough to check Eric's whereabouts on the night Hannah was killed.

Joaquin added, "If he grabbed Andrea and held her for three days before killing her, he might have been playing house with her. Following some kind of fantasy."

Or hurting her. He remembered ligature marks on the wrists. If the killer took captives, he needed a private place to hold them. "He didn't do that for Hannah. Or for Rene."

"He might have bonded with them. You know, singing a song together or dancing. He found ways to stay close to his victims that wouldn't make sense to anyone else."

Like Jackknife Jones driving Daisy in circles. "What else?"

"His motivations are complex," Joaquin said. "I'd be surprised to learn he's driven by a sexual fantasy. Instead, look for a psychologically unhealthy connection to his mother, sister or another close family member. A trigger incident with one of those women might jolt him into the need to commit murder. It's like he's rescuing them by killing them."

"What kind of incident?"

"Triggers might involve a death, a divorce, an argument or a separation. Mom might have divorced Dad and started a new family. The son would see murder as a way to keep Mom close."

"By killing other women?"

"There's a good deal of rage braided into his sadness and/or grief."

A twisted way of thinking. "What makes you study these perpetrators? What's the appeal in forensic psychology?"

"Maybe you should ask your new girlfriend, the biology teacher, why she studies corpses." Joaquin chuckled. "Call me after you have some results from the autopsy. I'll be interested in hearing about this investigation. And in meeting Daisy."

"Not that you've figured out who she is, what should I do about her?"

"Try chopping wood."

WHEN DAISY SLIPPED into the passenger seat of the NPS vehicle, she realized that her khaki skirt—a loose-fitting A-line—displayed a lot of leg, probably her best feature in the summer when she had a natural tan. She glanced over at Carter behind the steering wheel, tempted to explain that she'd chosen a skirt for her FBI interview so she'd look respectable, but then she'd also have to justify the black V-neck T-shirt that clung to her breasts under her lightweight brown jacket. Though she wasn't trying to look seductive, her outfit told a different story. Was she subconsciously putting out signals? Why else would she have blow-dried her curly blond hair into a smooth style that swooped gracefully across her forehead?

This was *not* a date. They'd drive to Pueblo, where she'd have an interview with the FBI and observe an autopsy. She had two other graveyards she wanted to check out as long as they were in the area. *Nothing romantic about any of those plans.*

Leaning back in her seat, she gazed through the windshield at a verdant June day with fluffy white clouds skipping across an azure sky. Fresh grasses dotted with crimson and blue wildflowers blanketed the valley below jagged red cliffs. The Arkansas River, flush with runoff from melted snow, cascaded beside the highway. On a day like this, when the late-morning breeze smelled like summer and sun, she easily understood why Carter loved living in the mountains instead of being a cop on the hot, dry, city streets of Denver.

She exhaled a quiet sigh. If they hadn't been hunting a serial killer, the day would have been perfect. "What did your profiler say about the crimes?"

"He has a theory based on the way the killer grooms and cares for the victims. It's almost as if he has an attachment to them."

"Then why would he kill them?"

"I talked to my supervisor about that. I'll tell you later." His eyebrows lowered in a scowl. "There was another issue with Andrea. According to SAC Wiley, she was reported missing on the fourteenth, but you placed time of death on the seventeenth or eighteenth. Where was she during those missing days?"

Daisy shuddered to think of the platinum blonde being held captive by the serial killer, especially since Andrea had known what had happened to her friend Hannah. Her body had been too mangled by predators to pinpoint signs of abuse, but there were ligature marks on her wrists and arms. "From her wounds, I can't tell if he hurt her..." She hesitated to use the word *torture*. "I didn't see scars or bruises indicating that he injured Rene. From what you told me about Hannah, her death came swiftly."

"Joaquin—my NPS Supervisor who used to be a psychologist—suggested that these weren't random killings. He stalks, pursues and captures women who have some kind of connection to him. Possibly he imagines affection—something he might feel for a family member, maybe even his mother." Carter groped for words to explain. "He might be using his victims as surrogates for women he felt close to. He might talk to them or sing to them."

Not surprisingly, the motivation for this serial killer also mystified her. Why would he do these terrible, degrading things? How could he think playing with his captives meant he cared for them? "I'm not great at putting myself into somebody else's head."

"Not when their thinking is so warped."

"But your supervisor knows forensic psychology. He studies perpetrators. What does that say about him?"

"I might ask the same of you. Why do you study dead people?" He gazed into her eyes, making a quick but deep connection. "For that matter, I must be as weird as you and Joaquin, because I like talking to both of you."

She continued to stare after he looked back at the road. In spite of herself, she wondered if he'd noticed how mascara brought out the green in her eyes. "Do you think I'm weird?"

"Not weird. I think you're extraordinary."

Definitely a first. No one had ever said that to her before. Uncomfortable, she wanted to get back to the business of investigating. "How can we use this profile?"

"When we're considering suspects, we should look for triggers—incidents involving his mother or a woman he was close to. What can you tell me about Eric Wolff?"

"He's not a killer," she protested. "He's a jealous, small-minded treasure hunter."

"He fits some parameters for the killer. He's the right age, has a job with flexible hours and can easily transport bodies in his van. He admitted to stalking you."

Every word he spoke rang true. She'd been disturbed when Eric confessed that he'd watched when Carter kissed her. Definitely a creep. But a serial killer?

"He lives in Pueblo with his father," she said. "His mother isn't in the picture. I think she left them when Eric was a teenager."

"Could be a trigger."

"But it happened a long time ago. Eric's in his thirties. Surely he's had time to get over being abandoned so many years ago."

"Some people never do. Early abandonment can scar a person for life."

"True." Her own upbringing as the only child of older parents had been relatively stable and free from tragedy. Not for the first time, she was thankful for being average. "What we should be asking is why now? What would activate Eric's early trauma?"

"We'll have to research his mother. She might be getting married to someone other than his father. Or she might have died."

"There's an easy way to verify if he was the killer or not," she said. "Check his alibi. Was he in Glenwood Springs when Hannah was killed? Or was that unverified?"

His mouth twisted in a wry grin. "I know why you're an anatomy whiz, but how do you know about alibis?"

"I read suspense novels," she said.

"Hannah was hanging out at a tavern with friends, including Andrea, and told them she was going to meet a guy who wanted to see the memorial to Doc Holliday. Could Eric pull that off?"

Slowly, she nodded. An awareness of danger spread through her. Her skin prickled. The first time she met Eric, he made a point of talking to her about cemeteries and the boot hill graveyards. He had convinced Aunt Vi to start looking for Sherwood Brighton's grave. Was Eric the killer?

A seed of fear had been planted in the back of her mind. During the two-and-a-half-hour drive, they discussed other suspects—including Slade Franklin, who also lived in Pueblo and was someone they'd visit while there. But she couldn't dismiss the thought of Eric Wolff stalking her through the forest.

When they got to the outskirts of Pueblo, she saw a dark blue van on the other side of the street, too far for her to make out the features of the driver. He drove out of sight before she could read the logo and see the image of paint cans. Was it him? Walking on the sidewalk, she saw a man who shuffled like Eric. This was his hometown. He could be anywhere. Waiting. Watching. Planning his attack.

Chapter Eight

The headquarters for the Pueblo branch of the FBI spread across the eighth and ninth floors of an office building around the corner from the Pueblo County Detention Center and the county sheriff's office. Daisy should have felt safe within these orderly corridors where cubicles and clusters of desks for field agents occupied open spaces and partitioned private offices lined the inner walls. Though these lawmen and women had locked their weapons away while in the office, they were equipped with the skill and training to protect her. Certainly they looked professional—most of the agents wore slacks and tucked-in shirts with blazers. Several had neckties.

A red-haired agent she recognized from the boot hill approached them and slapped Carter on the back in an aggressively friendly gesture. The agent was average height, but he appeared to be bigger due to the biceps bulging inside his shirtsleeves, giving the impression that if he flexed the seams would split. His striped necktie draped over his pecs and pointed toward his muscular thighs. When he shook Daisy's hand, she braced for a mighty grip and wasn't disappointed. She gritted her teeth to keep from flinching.

"Not sure we met at Butcher's Gulch," he said. "I'm Special Agent Mickey Hicks."

The guy with the cartoon character name. "I'm Daisy Brighton. Please call me Daisy."

"Sorry you got mixed up in this, Daisy, but don't you worry. We'll nab this guy."

She'd come here as a witness to give a statement, but Hicks's pale blue eyes seemed to accuse her. A sensation of undeserved guilt prickled across her skin like goose bumps. She hadn't done anything wrong but couldn't help but worry that some long-forgotten infraction would rise up and point an accusing finger in her direction.

Carter reintroduced her to SAC Pat Wiley, who was the opposite of Hicks. While Hicks was hard-edged and intense, Wiley reminded her of a pair of well-worn loafers—not pretty but exceedingly comfortable. He was average-looking with thinning brown hair, an easy grin and a bolo tie fastened with a circular silver slide etched with a howling coyote. *A wily coyote? Another cartoon?* His handshake reassured her, and so did his compliment—"Your analysis of the time of death seems to be right on target. We appreciate your assistance."

"I'm glad. But how did that help?"

"In the early part of the investigation, we gather as much information as possible on the actual crime. Your observations of insect larvae and the development of maggots caused you to place the time of death for these women at least two days apart. A significant detail."

A woman in a white lab coat, obviously a forensic investigator, picked her way through the desks and handed a folder to Hicks. Her tone was crisp. "DNA results confirm the identity of Rene Williams. By the way, you're welcome for the rush analysis."

Before Wiley could comment, she pivoted and left. Wiley ushered her and Carter into a small interrogation room with a table, four chairs and a two-way mirror on one wall. The space looked exactly as she expected from watching TV cop shows. Wiley gestured for her and Carter to sit on one side of the table while he took a chair opposite them, opened a fat envelope and took out a folder with forms, papers and photographs inside.

For a few moments, Carter and Wiley lobbed ideas back and forth, much the way she and Carter had on the drive. As far as she was concerned, this was unnecessary talk. The autopsy would provide information about whether the victim been restrained, raped or tortured. Carter opened a new direction to their speculation, asking about where Andrea might have been held. Did the killer live in the Glenwood Springs area where he'd met Andrea and Hannah? Or was Butcher's Gulch closer to his home base? Or was it totally unrelated to the victims? He might live in Pueblo.

Daisy lacked the ability to judge distances in the

mountains, which was why Jackknife had managed to drive her in circles. When the GPS on her phone went on the fritz, she was well and truly lost. The vast distances between towns and other areas heightened her respect for Carter's job. He didn't have as many violent crimes to investigate as a city cop, but his jurisdiction covered a wide and varied topography. Looking to Wiley, he said, "No matter where he lives, we'll need warrants to get your forensic investigators inside his truck or van."

"As soon as you give me cause, I'm on it." Wiley turned his head and pinned Daisy with a surprisingly sharp gaze. She figured he was deciding whether or not he should talk about the crime in her presence. "You might be more comfortable in the waiting room, Ms. Brighton."

"It's Daisy," she said. "And I don't mind hearing about your investigation."

"Having her observe is unorthodox," Carter said, "but she could be useful. The medical examiner has already agreed to let her attend the autopsies this afternoon."

"I'm impressed." Wiley arched an eyebrow. "Dr. Julia Stillwater doesn't break the rules for just anybody."

"Plus, Daisy is connected with two of the suspects—Jackknife Jones and Eric Wolff."

"Very well." Wiley adjusted his bolo tie and consulted a report from his folder. "I have information from the Glenwood Springs PD. They initiated their investigation into Andrea Lindstrom's disappearance after receiving a call from the insurance office where she worked. Her apartment showed no signs of being broken into. None of her friends or family had heard from her. The Glenwood cops were thorough. They didn't find any leads."

Daisy absorbed his words. Was Andrea grabbed off the street? Did the killer invite her to have a cup of coffee with him? Unlikely! No way would she engage in casual conversation with a stranger after what had happened to her friend Hannah. "I wonder if she drove home after work on the day before she went missing. Where was her car?"

"In a grocery store parking lot."

A clear picture formed in her mind. "I'll bet her shopping bags were half loaded into the trunk."

"Good hunch," Wiley said. "How did you know that?"

"I'm a single woman who tries to be cautious. When I get out of my car, I hold the vial of pepper spray on my key chain, cocked and ready to fire. I don't even think about the pepper spray anymore. It's habit." Though not aware of being nervous, her voice cracked. She cleared her throat. "I'm most vulnerable when I'm in the middle of unloading stuff and my arms are full."

Under the table, Carter took her hand and gently squeezed. She hoped he didn't feel her trembling.

"Good reasoning," Wiley said. "That's pretty much what the Glenwood cops concluded."

"I liked working with those detectives," Carter said. "What else did they find?"

"Hannah Guerrero had a connection with Pueblo. Her great-uncle died in October of last year, and she attended the funeral at Rolling Hills Cemetery."

Daisy's ears pricked up. That cemetery was on her list of places where Sherwood Brighton could be buried. "Where is that located?"

"South Pueblo. I can give you directions." He flipped a page in his folder. "That evening, she went jogging along the Riverwalk."

The few bits of information she recalled about Hannah included her occupation as a dental assistant and her high level of physical fitness. An evening jog made sense, and the Riverwalk was a charming location where the wide Arkansas River curled through the center of town. Elegantly landscaped, the sprawling acreage housed a selection of shops and restaurants. The renovations represented an integral part of Pueblo's transformation from the so-called Steel City to an artsy community with galleries, concerts and a ballet company.

"On that very same night," Wiley said, "the body of a young woman was found among the trees at the north edge of the Riverwalk. Not a well-lighted area, but she was visible from the sidewalk where Hannah and other joggers would have been running. The victim had been arranged with her back against a thick tree trunk. At first, an observer might think she was taking a break from her stroll and resting while she peacefully watched the river roll by."

"How cold was it?" Daisy asked.

"In early evening, around fifty or fifty-five. The victim wore a light jacket and jeans."

He took an eight-by-ten photo from the folder and slid it across the table to Carter, who shared the picture with her. Daisy agreed with Wiley's statement about the victim appearing to be resting. His next photo showed heavy bruising around her throat. *Strangled.*

The method of killing differed from the three women in the current investigation, but the way the body had been arranged echoed the Butcher's Gulch murderer's careful display of his victims. She wasn't an expert on criminal behavior, but the appearance of another dead woman who was connected with Hannah had to be more than coincidence. "Did Hannah find the body?"

"She didn't report it but was definitely in the area."

Though she and Carter had discovered the most recent victims, the roots of these serial killings stretched back farther into the past. Could there have been others? How many? She imagined an endless queue of young women clutching their throats with their eyes closed in death and their mouths gaping open in silent screams.

Goose bumps broke out on her arms. She might

already have met this killer, might have heard his voice and inhaled the smell of bloodlust clinging to him. Would she know him when he came close? Or would he blend in, indistinguishable until he attacked?

Her chills solidified in a frozen lump in her chest, making it hard to breathe. She groped for Carter's hand, needing his strength and reassurance, but he was leaning across the table toward Wiley, his gaze intense. His voice took on an avid tone. "Is it unusual for a serial killer to change his method of murder?"

"It happens." Wiley shrugged. "He's still defining himself."

"What about the scarf?" Carter asked. "The woman on the Riverwalk wasn't wearing a scarf."

A photograph of a silver necklace with a heart pendant joined the other two pictures on the table. "None of her friends or family recognized the necklace she was wearing. He crushed her throat with so much force that the chain embedded in her skin. A reenactment of the crime based on forensic evidence indicated that he stood behind her, perhaps fastening the heart necklace at her nape before he choked her."

"Strangulation is nowhere near as messy as a slicing an artery and seems less efficient," Carter said. "Why change?"

"We can agree that he's an organized killer who plans every detail and doesn't leave much to chance. Strangling might seem tidy, but a victim who's being choked is more likely to fight."

"Not if he grabs them from behind," Carter said.

"She might kick, might throw herself on the ground or break away and cry for help."

Daisy felt the blood drain from her face. Studying the deceased didn't bother her but hearing about the struggle before death set her imagination racing down a dark, dangerous pathway. She seldom went to horror movies. And when the scary music started playing, she covered her eyes and gritted her teeth so she wouldn't scream. "Are there others? How long has he been killing?"

"I'm waiting to get more information," Wiley said. "The Riverwalk victim came from the Southern Ute Reservation near Durango. The investigation was taken over by tribal police."

Carter nodded. "I've never had a problem dealing with the tribes."

"That's because you're a ranger, a protector of the forests. They don't see you as the enemy. You'd be surprised by how many people resent the FBI and don't want to cooperate."

Daisy understood that reluctance. Moments ago, when she entered the offices of the all-powerful FBI, she'd been nervous, expecting to be arrested for a forgotten crime, something so minor that she didn't remember. The tribal police had reason to distrust the feds, stemming from a history of broken treaties and land grabs. She could understand why they'd prefer to work with an investigative ranger like Carter who shared their respect for the land.

"In any case," Wiley said, "we're expanding our computer search to include young women who were missing or killed in the past ten years."

An endless line of victims... Unable to cope with the idea of so much fear—terror from the murdered women who knew they were about to die and from her own deep-seated nightmares—Daisy went silent while Carter and Wiley continued to discuss the investigation.

In her imagination, the murderer evolved into a monster with blood dripping from his fangs and his fingernails sharpened into talons. *Ridiculous.* According to science, the natural world contained many horrifying creatures, including the apex predators at the top of the food chain. Great white sharks, Burmese pythons and grizzlies were virtual killing machines. Horrifying and lethal but predictable, they didn't frighten her as much as an innocent-looking individual who lured his prey into danger. She wanted this serial killer caught. At the same time, she realized there wasn't much she could do to find and arrest a murderer. Daisy hadn't trained as an investigator.

As soon as they were done at the FBI office, she and Carter would observe the autopsy. A much better use of her skills.

Chapter Nine

As they approached the autopsy suite, Carter trained his watchful gaze on Daisy. In her short skirt with her practical hiking boots, her tanned legs provided a sexy distraction from his concerns about her state of mind. She'd told him repeatedly that she was fine. Her posture and athletic gait showed the confidence he'd come to expect from her. But when she reached up and brushed a shiny wing of blond hair off her forehead, she avoided looking at him. She'd been jumpy since they left Leadville. During their time with SAC Wiley in the interrogation room, her nervousness had increased. The roses in her cheeks faded to ash. Her hands trembled.

He didn't understand. He'd watched this woman calmly examine maggots on a corpse and lean close to check the wounds. But talking about the investigation had her rattled. When they got down to the official business of Wiley taking her witness statement for the record, she'd regained some of her poise, especially when she discussed the injuries on the victims.

What's she hiding? Every time he asked if she was okay, she said the same thing: "Fine." He didn't think she was lying. Why would she? But there was definitely something she wasn't telling him.

He paused outside the autopsy area and asked, "Are you sure you want to do this?"

"I've been looking forward to watching Dr. Julia Stillwater work." When she gazed up at him, her green eyes widened. Her smile seemed genuine. "She's a legend. According to one of my former profs, there's nobody better than Dr. Stillwater. She's done tremendous work on facial reconstruction."

Though he believed her enthusiasm, he still saw tension. "Maybe we should grab a cup of coffee before we go inside."

"I'd rather watch."

Actually, he wouldn't mind another coffee. Last night, he hadn't slept, and it was almost lunchtime. "Are you hungry?"

"I'm fine."

Fine. He was beginning to hate that word. Because she wasn't fine. She was frightened, on edge. "Something's bothering you, and I want to know what it is."

"Nothing, really."

He had no choice but to follow her into a carpeted waiting area with its functional chairs and tables. The boring furniture was where the resemblance to other institutional settings ended. An abstract painting of the high desert landscape covered the walls in turquoise, gold, sienna and purple—colors associated with the Southwest. Leafy plants, like dieffenbachia, dragon tree and that one with the spidery leaves, ranged around the room in terra cotta pots, also painted with colorful geometric designs. A sign that said Autopsy marked the wall beside a windowed door. On the opposite side was the forensic laboratory. Haunting melodies from a wooden flute shimmered in the background.

"Mellow." Daisy's tension took a giant step toward calm. "This decor has got to be from the earth mother influence of Julia Stillwater."

He'd only met the doctor in person once before and had never attended an autopsy, but he respected her knowledge and had immediately liked this strong Ute tribal elder who supervised a clinic on the reservation in addition to her work as a medical examiner.

In the anteroom outside the large area where the actual autopsies would be performed, an intern in scrubs wearing a Harley-Davidson surgical cap and a black N95 mask took their names and directed them to the area where they could change into hats, booties, gloves, masks and disposable suits to cover their clothes.

While she got dressed in the sanitary gear, Daisy asked, "Have they started the autopsy?"

"They're still doing the external exam." The intern shrugged. "What's the deal with these victims? There's a whole bunch of observers."

Carter expected as much. There would be agents from the FBI, state police and the coroner for

Pueblo County, at the very least. "It's a possible serial killer."

The intern's dark brown eyes were his only visible feature. He squeezed them closed and then open, an expression that could have meant surprise, excitement or just about anything else. "Whoa."

"Has the autopsy uncovered any forensic data, like a tox screen?"

"There was one done, but I don't have the details." He bobbed his head. "The only thing Doc Julia said was that the suggested time of death was within reasonable parameters."

Daisy nudged his arm. "Did you hear that? I'm within reasonable parameters."

They entered the autopsy room, where two stainless steel tables with gutters on either side were set up in the midst of other equipment, including measuring devices, scalpels, forceps, shears, saws and other tools he didn't recognize. Dr. Julia Stillwater turned the naked body of Rene Williams onto her side to display the dark purpling of lividity on her back and torso. One intern held the body in place while another took photos.

Behind her plastic face shield, the doctor wore a recording microphone headset. She motioned to the intern with the camera and pointed to the grayish flesh of Rene's arm. "Butterfly tattoo above the ligature marks on her left wrist. Where there's one, often there are more."

With the intern snapping photos, they recorded

five other tats, including a horoscope sign for Scorpio and an arrangement of stars that looked like the Big Dipper. Carter looked away from the dead woman. Instead, he focused on the doctor as she moved in a methodical manner from the top of Rene's head to her feet, from her fingertips to her shoulders. Once again, they turned her onto her stomach. With precision, the doctor and her interns recorded all the visible scratches, bruises and wounds.

"Make sure you get a photo of that double puncture," she said, indicating an area on the victim's side. "Those marks either came from a stun gun or she was attacked by a vampire."

The investigators, including Carter, focused on this new revelation. He was fairly sure that Hannah hadn't been hit by a stun gun, which meant the killer had made another change in his procedure. Had he also zapped Andrea?

On Rene's upper back above the shoulder blade, Dr. Stillwater found the final tattoo. The name *Josh* surrounded by a heart. Josh Santana was the boyfriend. Another suspect.

Glancing around the room, Carter counted seven other observers. None were as keenly interested as Daisy, who kept inching closer to the examination table for a better look. When the intern who had been taking photos stepped back, the doctor picked up her scalpel. The overhead surgical lights flashed against the silver blade. The time had come for the

Y-shaped incision that would lay the organs bare. Not Carter's idea of a good time.

Behind her plastic face shield, Julia Stillwater grinned at Daisy. "Are you Ms. Brighton?"

"It's an honor to meet you, Doctor."

"You're a biology teacher."

"That's right."

"Good job estimating time of death. We should talk."

"I'd like that."

Carter couldn't see Daisy's mouth behind her mask, but he knew she was smiling from ear to ear. The doctor ranked high in her estimation, and the mere thought of a chat about forensic medicine had wiped away her fears and nervousness. She'd recalibrated her mood. Now, she was really and truly, actually *fine*.

On the other hand, he wasn't altogether thrilled to be here. To be sure, he wanted and needed the forensic evidence that would be revealed when Dr. Stillwater cracked open the rib cage and cut through Rene Williams's breastbone. The doc would discover all kinds of useful details when she removed the major organs and analyzed them. Ditto for the brain.

But he really wasn't interested in the procedure. He didn't care how she reached her conclusions, didn't need to see or smell the actual stomach contents. It was enough for him to read the autopsy report and learn what Rene had eaten for her last meal.

While he searched his mind for a plausible excuse to leave the autopsy, Dr. Stillwater saved him the trouble. She returned her scalpel to the sanitary tray and stepped back from the table. "I think I'll take a break now. Half an hour or so. For those of you who are observing, don't touch the body. Feel free to visit the cafeteria for coffee or tea. Remember to suit up again when you return. Daisy, please come with me."

When she turned and strode from the room, her interns carefully covered the naked body and the surgical tools. Daisy hurried out the door and down the hallway after her idol, and Carter followed.

DAISY'S EXPECTATIONS FOR the office of an earth mother who was also a scientist were happily met when they entered a large room with two tall windows. Long wooden planter boxes filled with basil, peas and peppers stretched beneath each window and were bathed in sunlight. Tendrils of ivy dripped over the edges and touched the floor. In the corner, a big-leafed bird-of-paradise plant reached all the way to the ceiling. A set of bookshelves held intricately painted bowls and vases from the Ute Mountain pottery collection as well as woven baskets. Family photos and artwork done by grandchildren decorated the walls. A casual clutter of papers, folders and books kept the place from looking like a museum.

A small desk—stacked with incoming work—lurked in the corner, while a long, polished walnut table surrounded by comfortable chairs dominated the center of the room. Dr. Stillwater peeled off her protective gear, revealing turquoise scrubs and two long black braids that had been tucked inside her cap. She went to another table and filled the reservoir in a coffee maker with distilled water. "You'll both have coffee," she said. "Feel free to take off the gowns, gloves and masks."

As Carter stripped off the outer layer of sanitary clothing, he thanked her for her hospitality. "We've met before," he said.

"I remember you, Ranger. It's Aloysius Periwinkle Carter, isn't it?"

Aloysius Periwinkle? Daisy squelched the urge to poke fun. She'd been teased about her name that seemed to rhyme with everything, including crazy, lazy and—worst of all—easy.

"A. P. Carter IV." A sheepish grin curled his lips. "You have a good memory."

"I keep track of people who interest me." She ground the beans from a canister and set the coffee to brew. The aroma mingled with the pleasant, herbaceous scent of the room. "You've worked with tribal police more than once."

"I have respect for the men and women who

keep order on the rez. I hope to talk with them about a murder that took place last October."

Daisy remembered the victim found at the Riverwalk. "Is that killing related to these two autopsies?"

"I believe so," he said. "The victim was strangled."

"Eileen Findlay," Dr. Julia said. "I did the autopsy. Give my assistant her name, and she'll pull the files." She turned her dark-eyed gaze on Daisy. "Tell me how a biology teacher from Denver ends up in a graveyard outside a ghost town."

"Ever heard of Brighton's Bullion?"

"The golden treasure."

Not wanting to waste much time on the family myth, Daisy rushed through her explanation of why she'd been searching for the grave of the outlaw Sherwood Brighton. "We found the gravestone for his wife, Annie, at Butcher's Gulch. I don't know why this respectable woman was buried in an outlaws' cemetery, but she was."

"A mystery," Dr. Julia said. "I heard that you encourage your high school students to work with cadavers."

"I don't get to provide that experience as often as I'd like. Sometimes, there aren't bodies available. Sometimes, parents refuse permission." She was always surprised when the adults wouldn't allow their children to participate. "When studying anatomy, it's best to see a real-life example of how organs fit together—and work together—in the body. I also have botany classes where I make the students start a garden. I mean, how can they understand plants when they think all produce comes prepackaged from a grocery store?"

"You're a good teacher." Dr. Julia took both of her hands and held them, making a connection. "If you ever consider leaving Denver, there's a place for you here."

Stunned into silence, Daisy absorbed this special moment in time. The warmth of Dr. Julia's touch. The scent of earth from plants and coffee. The colors and patterns of the Ute designs. She glanced at Carter, realizing that he fit precisely into this picture, these feelings.

She cleared her throat. "Thank you."

"I mean it." Dr. Julia gave her hands a squeeze and returned to her coffee maker. She filled three ceramic mugs that bore stylized sunrise designs. "We have a strong community of scientists and artists. We can use someone with your skills. And your passion."

Daisy would love to work with this plainspoken woman who was also brilliant. "I read your paper on the advantages of the Rokitansky method in organ removal during autopsy, and I agree with your conclusion about how it's important to take your time."

"Even when you have a room full of officers who

are anxious to hear results." She aimed a sidelong glance at Carter. "Those are your people, Ranger."

"I try not to be impatient," he said, "but you can always bluff me because I don't understand anatomy. If you told me it took a week to study the spleen, I wouldn't contradict. I don't even know where to find the spleen."

The doctor's laughter sounded as rich as her coffee tasted. Daisy's spirits lightened. "Maybe you can help me understand something. Scientific explanations make sense to me, and I can happily study forensics all day. But when it comes to speculation and deduction, I'm totally confused."

"Give me an example."

"When Carter talks about the investigation and starts posing theories. I imagine the serial killer as a predator—which, to tell the truth, he is. And I scare myself."

"You need solid facts to be grounded. I'm much the same. My brain works deductively. For example, I saw twin puncture marks on Rene's side below the rib cage. My deduction—she had been incapacitated by a stun gun. That's a rational conclusion. Factual."

Daisy completely understood. She looked to Carter for his opinion. "What do you think about the puncture marks?"

"I'm wondering why he used it. When did he zap her—when he first captured her or right before he killed her? Did he use the gun on his other victims? There was no mention of puncture wounds in Hannah's autopsy report." He focused on Dr. Julia. "I'll be interested to hear about the victim from the reservation. Maybe Hannah was an outlier and he didn't stun her because he knew they were completely alone."

"So much speculation." Daisy sipped her coffee. "And no way of knowing the truth. I'm already imagining this monster terrorizing the women he killed. How can we ever know why?"

"Psychology and profiling." Carter looked to Dr. Julia. "I spoke to Joaquin Stanley."

"How is the old hippie?"

"Same as always."

On the drive down here, Carter had outlined his supervisor's profile of the murderer. They should look for an organized killer who was not sexually motivated. A stalker, he was fond of his victims and might develop an attachment to them. Probably, he was triggered by a traumatic event involving a woman he cared about, i.e., mother, sister, grandmother, friend.

After he ran down the same list with Dr. Julia, she gazed across the rim of her coffee mug at Daisy. "In my culture, there is a belief that the recently dead become ghostwalkers and stay close to the body for a period of time. The killer might believe he is resurrecting a relationship that died."

She shuddered. Adding ghosts to her imagination didn't help. She dragged them back to facts.

"One of our suspects admitted to stalking me. Should I worry? Am I in danger?"

"Stalking might be a part of the serial killer's procedure," Dr. Julia said, "but there are others who stalk for other reasons. Either way, it's a threatening behavior. That's a fact."

"Got it. I should take steps to protect myself from this guy."

"We might learn more from studying victimology. Again, based on fact. Killers are more likely to attack when the victim is unprotected or in a dangerous place."

Daisy thought of Hannah being drawn to the memorial, where she'd be alone. Andrea had been grabbed in a grocery store parking lot, where she was not alone but surrounded by people who were distracted by their own business. "What else?"

"Trust no one. Avoid risky behavior. And—this is really important—align yourself with a suitable guardian."

"Like Carter." She was still frightened but doubted she'd be injured when he was with her. "No more visiting cemeteries by myself, especially after dark."

Dr. Julia asked, "Do you have any specific reason to believe you might be targeted as the next victim?"

She shook her head. "Just my overactive imagination."

"There is something," Carter said. "We're examining links between these women. Hannah was at the Riverwalk when the Ute woman was killed. Andrea was a friend of Hannah's. Rene was close to the place where Andrea was dumped after she was murdered."

"I'm not part of those connections," Daisy said. "Maybe you should keep an eye on Pinkie and the other women at the party who were friends of Rene."

"Good idea," he said. "I'll mention it to the FBI."

Dr. Julia stood and drained her coffee mug. "Time for me to go back to work. Daisy, would you like to assist with the rest of the autopsy?"

"Absolutely."

She bounced to her feet as though her legs were on springs. Eager didn't begin to describe her enthusiasm. Without thinking she gave Carter a hug and a friendly kiss on the cheek. *Whoa, girl, that's not smart.* No matter how hard she tried to keep their relationship nonphysical, her natural impulses kept pushing her toward him.

Settling his cowboy hat on his head, he gazed at her from under the brim. His blue eyes shimmered. His lips curved in one of his sexy smiles while he informed her that he needed to check in at the FBI office and would return for her in an hour or so. "I might try to meet with Slade Franklin while we're in town."

She remembered the clean-cut, tall man from the party. Talking to him at Butcher's Gulch hadn't frightened her before. But now? When everybody was a suspect? It might be good for her to confront him again. "If you don't mind, I'd like to come along when you interview Slade."

He cocked his head to one side. "Why?"

"To face my fears."

"Shouldn't be a problem for you to come along." He gave her arm a squeeze. "I'll be back. Don't go anywhere else without me."

She watched the office door close behind him. For her, talking to a suspect—even someone who seemed as innocent as Slade—marked a step in the right direction. She'd treat this interview like a science experiment, separating facts from imagination. And she'd follow Dr. Julia's advice: find the verifiable truth and do everything possible to avoid risk.

Chapter Ten

After spending an hour and a half at FBI headquarters, Carter returned to pick up Daisy, who was waiting for him outside the autopsy suite. Bubbling over, she delighted in telling him every detail about the autopsy on their walk to his SUV, starting with how she and Dr. Julia had removed the organs from the body cavity, weighed them and prepared slides for further examination. According to their preliminary findings, Rene Williams had been a healthy young woman who should have lived a long life. As Daisy spoke those words, her voice quavered slightly, which might have been the first time he'd seen her show emotion about a dead person.

"It's difficult to imagine," she said, underlining this deviation from her usual detachment, "the loss of a young life. She'll never marry, never have children, never have a chance to fulfill her dreams. I wonder what she was studying in college."

He rested his hand on her shoulder, offering comfort. The cruelty, the injustice and the sorrow of every murder case he'd investigated—from his years as a cop in Denver to his career as a ranger—touched him. He'd given up trying to keep himself uninvolved and impersonal. When he thought of Rene, Andrea and Hannah, he experienced the loss and the pain. "The FBI contacted her parents. They live on a ranch in Wyoming."

"I can't imagine what this is like for them."

"Neither can I."

She paused outside the passenger door of his SUV and gazed up at him. "I haven't let you get a word in edgewise. What else is happening with the feds?"

"Forensics has a couple of clear footprints for size-thirteen shoes. The same size was found near Hannah's crime scene."

"Is that an unusual size?"

"Not really. I wear a twelve, and I'm six foot three."

"Anything else?" she asked.

"When you saw Andrea's body, you said it must have been covered or hidden so the predators wouldn't completely tear her apart. And you were correct. Forensics found scraps and fibers." He paused before revealing more. This fact might send her spiraling down the wrong path. But what was he going to do—lie to her? "The scraps come from white canvas, the kind of material that painters—or carpenters—use."

"A drop cloth?"

He knew what she was thinking. "Don't make too much of this. It's likely that Eric Wolff has drop cloths as part of his regular equipment. And Slade probably uses them when he applies finish on wood products."

"Drop cloths are inexpensive and common. I've bought them myself when I painted my kitchen." Her forehead crinkled in a frown. "Those scraps might point toward Eric, but the cloth doesn't count as a valid clue unless we find it and it's stained with blood."

"And that's just about everything I learned from the feds. Wiley was happy when I gave him a copy of Dr. Julia's autopsy report for Eileen Findlay, the woman who was found at the Riverwalk. She grew up on the Southern Ute Reservation but lived in Pueblo, where she was a student at CSU. He's working on possible connections between her and Hannah."

"Other than Hannah stumbling over her body?"

"Yep." He pushed his hat off his forehead and tilted his face toward the sun. The warmth of early summer eased the chill from the autopsy suite. Outdoors, they were surrounded by life. Robins and wrens chirped from the trees. People rushed along the sidewalks. Afternoon sunlight glittered against his windshield. Though he and Daisy had already accomplished a lot today, it was only half past four. There was more to be done. "Before we go to the graveyards you want to explore, I'd like to pay a visit to Slade Franklin."

"The guy with the buzz cut who we met at Butcher's Gulch. The carpenter who might use drop cloths. Is he a suspect?"

"It's worth talking to him. He was one of the last

people to see Rene alive, and he drives a camper truck that could be used to transport victims."

"Does he have a criminal record?"

"He's squeaky clean." Which made Agent Wiley think Slade was an unlikely suspect. Interviewing him ranked as low priority. "I called his cell phone, and he agreed to meet at his house in fifteen minutes. Lucky timing. He's not working today until he has an appointment to give a bid on a project at half past five."

"What kind of project?"

"Some kind of renovation." He opened the passenger-side door for her. "The way I figure, we have enough time to talk with him and drive to one of your cemeteries before nightfall."

He got behind the steering wheel and plugged the address into his GPS. Even though he was one hundred percent mountain man, he appreciated the convenience of cell phones and other technology. He glanced over at Daisy, who was nibbling on her lower lip. Holding back words?

She piped up. "Do you mind if I tell you more about the autopsy?"

His jaw clenched. He'd really heard enough, but this was important to her...and she was important to him. "I'm listening."

She tried to keep her explanation technical but he understood the whole disturbing picture. "While studying the brain, Dr. Julia discovered evidence of a concussion, probably caused by blunt-force trauma."

"Was she unconscious before he killed her?"

"I can't say with full accuracy, but probably."

"And so," he said, drawing his own conclusion, "the killer rendered her unconscious, either by blunt-force trauma or by zapping her with a stun gun. He really wanted to keep Rene from feeling pain."

She nodded. "Is that significant?"

"Could be." He thought of Joaquin's profile that presumed the serial killer had a fondness for his victims and tried to take care of them. If he was living out a twisted fantasy about a former loved one, he wouldn't want to hurt her…not even when he slashed her throat.

"When we're talking to Slade," she asked, "is there any sort of protocol? You know, like I could be the good cop and you could be the bad."

"Just be yourself." The idea of Daisy impersonating any sort of officer amused him. Though she radiated a certain amount of authority as a teacher, she lacked aggression. "You're too well mannered to be a hardened cop."

In less than fifteen minutes, he parked at the curb outside a Craftsman-style house in an older neighborhood. Yellow with white trim, a second floor, a neatly mowed lawn and a clump of juniper bushes beside the detached garage, the house didn't look like the home of a thirtysomething single man. Too tidy. The chairs on the front porch were old lady rockers with flower-patterned cushions instead of sturdy Adirondacks where a guy could sprawl and have a beer. Slade's truck with the camper on the back was parked in the driveway.

That vehicle was one of the main reasons Carter wanted another interview. An important piece of the serial killer's MO involved driving from place to place, transporting his victims. If Carter discovered sufficient reason to suspect Slade, he'd get a warrant for the FBI forensic team to process the truck camper, looking for blood, fibers and DNA.

As he and Daisy strolled up the sidewalk to the front door, the screen door swung open and Slade stepped out. "Nice to see you, sir. And you, too, ma'am."

Though he was thirty-one, two years older than Daisy, Slade came across as younger. Long-limbed and skinny, he looked like he hadn't filled out. Though he had the beginnings of wrinkles at the corners of his eyes and his mouth, his features seemed unformed. His clothes—a short-sleeved cotton shirt tucked into beige chinos—looked totally inoffensive.

After Daisy shook his hand, she asked, "What kind of carpentry do you do?"

"I like renovations, fixing up run-down houses." He ran his hand across his brown buzz cut. "I really like tearing out old stuff. Demolition can be pretty dang cool."

Not a guy who used profanity, especially not in front of a lady. Carter suspected he'd been well trained. A stern mother? "We have a couple of follow-up questions. May we come inside?"

"Just one thing." Slade lowered his voice. "I'd appreciate it if you didn't mention that me and Rene spent time alone together."

"Why not?"

"My girlfriend is in the kitchen, and she gets jealous."

A girlfriend? Mentally, Carter moved him several rungs lower on the suspect list. Typically, serial killers weren't able to maintain relationships. "What's her name?"

"Brandi Thoreau."

"How long have you dated?"

"Off and on for a couple of years."

"Wait a minute," Daisy said. "I thought you broke up with her."

"I did." He winced. "Rene is the person who encouraged me to get back together with Brandi. She understood what love was all about, and I owe her for that. I'm sad that she died."

Carter wanted to correct this sugary remembrance to include the word *murder*, which was the most important detail about Rene's death. But the hangdog expression on Slade's face gave him pause. Carter empathized with the guy. Did Slade empathize? If so, that emotion represented another sign that he wasn't a serial killer.

In the living room, Carter settled into a patterned gray chair that matched the sofa and love seat. Not the furniture a young man would choose. Nor would he select the paint-by-numbers versions of landscape paintings. In the attached dining room, an upright piano stood by the inner wall and a breakfront displayed a collection of blue-and-white-patterned plates and bowls that could have belonged to Carter's prim and proper grandmother—one of the few adults in his family that he actually liked.

An unexpected fragrance tickled the inside of his nose. "What's that smell?"

Slade shrugged. "Some weed that grows wild in the backyard. Not marijuana, though."

"English lavender," Daisy said. "I have some growing in my yard in Denver. The fragrance reminds me of rosemary. It's native to Colorado. When you dry the stems, crumble them up and add a couple of essential oils, you have a great potpourri. Did you make this yourself?"

"Brandi did it," he said. "Come to think of it, Mama loves the smell. She puts the lavender into tiny, silky bags and tucks it into her dresser drawers."

"Sachets." Daisy perched at the edge of the love seat. If she was frightened, she wasn't showing any signs of nervousness. "You have a lovely home. Very cozy."

The swinging door to the kitchen opened, and

a busty brunette in a sparkly, sleeveless tank top and skinny jeans charged through. She was a short woman in high heels. "Really?" she demanded. "Do you really think this old crap is lovely?"

Always polite, Daisy stood, faced the young lady and introduced herself. "You must be Brandi."

"That's right." Brandi shook her hand. "What do you really think about this ancient furniture? Those creepy old dishes?"

"Not my favorite style," Daisy said, "but a lot of people like the classics."

"Classic crap." Brandi rolled her big brown eyes and adjusted her long, bouncy ponytail. Her hair was an unusual reddish-brown like mahogany. "Slade's mama liked this cheesy junk. And he hasn't seen fit to get rid of it."

"Does his mother live here?"

"This was her house. He moved back home to take care of her after she had a stroke."

Slade stepped up beside her. Standing over six feet, he nearly matched Carter's height, and he towered over Brandi. "Mama loved her dishes and chairs."

"But Mama has been dead for two years." She planted her little fists on her hips and glared up at him. "Honey, it's time to let go."

Daisy shot Carter a glance, and he nodded. This circumstance—the recent death of a beloved mother—might trigger a serial killer.

"Okay, sweetheart." Slade smoothed her hair off

her forehead. "Next week, we'll go shopping, and you can help me pick out dishes."

Carter introduced a different topic. "Let's talk about your work. You're an independent contractor, right?"

"There are builders and remodelers I work with a lot, but I'm my own boss." He sounded proud about the arrangement. "I like being able to plan my own schedule."

A telling comment if he was the serial killer. "Did you ever have a regular employer?"

"Before I moved back to Pueblo, I worked full-time for a builder in Denver, and he taught me a lot. He also advised me to do an apprenticeship and join the union so I could earn top dollar. All I ever wanted to do was work with wood."

"Did your father teach you the basics?" Carter asked.

Slade scoffed. His voice took on an uncharacteristic bitterness. "He left when I was five years old. I haven't seen my old man ever since."

Carter was curious about the woman who raised him as a single mother but doubted he'd get an accurate picture from Slade, who cared so much about Mama that he couldn't get rid of her furniture. Or from Brandi, who probably hadn't liked the woman and resented the hold she still had on Slade. Might be useful to talk to a neighbor.

"My honey-boo is a really good carpenter." Brandi stroked the smooth parquet top of the coffee table in front of the sofa. “He did this, and it’s gorgeous. I think he ought to open a store to sell custom furniture.”

“Well, sweetheart, it sounds like you’ve got all kinds of plans for how I ought to spend my money.”

“It’s not like you’re broke. Mama left you big bucks.” Brandi glanced toward Daisy. “The old lady was rich. Not super-rich, but she had enough that she never needed to work.”

“Don’t make it sound like she was lazy.” Once again, Slade’s voice was bitter.

“Oh, I forgot. Mama was perfect.”

Before the conversation turned into a spat, Daisy stepped in. “Brandi, my throat’s dry. May I have a glass of water?”

“Sure thing.” She pivoted on her extra-high heels. “Come with me to the kitchen.”

Slade watched them go, and Carter watched Slade as his expression changed from a scowl to a grin. Totally appropriate if he was eyeballing his girlfriend. But he said, “Daisy is really something. Real ladylike. You’d better hang on to her.”

“I intend to.” *So back off.*

He exhaled a sigh. “I sure wish Brandi had spent more time with Mama. Some of her classy attitude might have rubbed off.”

“Tell me about your mama. What was her name?”

“Elizabeth Hotchkiss Franklin. She never went by Lizzy or Beth. Always her full name. Elizabeth." He strolled over to a built-in bookshelf below the staircase and picked up a photograph, framed in simple gold. "She was a beauty, slender and graceful. And always well-dressed."

He held the eight-by-ten photo so Carter could see. The picture had been taken outside a wrought iron gate fitted with a weathered brass plaque for Rolling Hills Cemetery and showed a younger version of Slade in a dark suit and black necktie. His long arm wrapped around the shoulders of a dark-haired woman who almost matched his height.

"Doesn't she look great!" Slade said. "She made that dress herself."

Clean and stylish, they looked like they'd come from the funeral of an important person. Elizabeth wore an elegant, fitted black dress with long sleeves.

Tied around her throat was a silky scarf decorated with green and blue swirls.

IN THE KITCHEN, Daisy recognized more homey touches that had likely been passed down from Mama. The salt and pepper shakers on the drop-leaf wood table were a chicken and a rooster. Some of the tiles on the backsplash behind the sink showed a Dutch boy and girl kissing. The light wood cabinetry, however, was modern and beautifully made, probably more of Slade's work.

Brandi lifted a bottle from an array of liquors on a cabinet beside the fridge. She unscrewed the top. "Would you like a taste of something more interesting than water?"

"What is it?"

"White rum. Tastes like raisins."

Though she had no desire to get blitzed, Daisy figured one drink wouldn't make a difference, and the alcohol might loosen Brandi's tongue. "Yes, please. On the rocks."

"Slade tells me you're a schoolteacher." She scooped ice from the fridge into two short, clear glasses and splashed in a healthy dose of clear rum. "I used to think I wanted to do that."

"What changed your mind?"

"School bored the pants off me." Brandi handed a glass to Daisy. "And I figured I could make more money as an online influencer. I do vlogs—that's a blog but mostly video—and podcasts about makeup and clothes and shopping."

Her occupation explained the sparkly top—an outfit too fancy for loafing around the house. "You must know a lot about computers."

"Abso-flipping-lutely." She clinked her glass against Daisy's, took a healthy sip and tossed her head, sending ripples through her mahogany-brown ponytail. "So, Miss Schoolteacher, are you going to tell me why you and your boyfriend—who is majorly cute, by the way—are here talking to Slade?"

"Just putting together more details for the investigation."

"Nope, I'm not buying that." Brandi took another slug. "Is Slade a suspect? Should I hire a lawyer for him?"

"Do you think he needs one?"

"Hmm." Again, she rolled her eyes, which must be her go-to expression. "Do I think my sweetie pie boyfriend is a serial killer? No way in hell. Why are you here?"

Daisy took a ladylike sip of rum. Not her favorite drink, but she didn't mind the astringent burn as the liquid coursed down her gullet and splashed into her empty stomach. She hadn't eaten since they arrived in Pueblo, except for an energy bar Dr. Julia had given her. "If Slade was seriously under suspicion, do you think the FBI would send me and Ranger Carter to talk with him?"

"Never thought of that." She drained her glass and gave herself a refill. "You two aren't high-ranking interrogators. Not to be insulting, but the feds would know better than to have a schoolmarm chasing Ted Bundy. Am I right?"

"You are."

"But maybe you're undercover FBI. That would be so cool."

"But not true," Daisy said emphatically. "Things are usually exactly as they seem. For example, your boyfriend doesn't fit the profile. Serial killers don't usually have girlfriends."

"But he's weird about Mama," she admitted. "That's a serial killer thing, right?"

"Could be."

"I'm so totally glad the old lady was so much taller than me."

Daisy finished off her rum. "Why?"

"Slade keeps trying to get me to dress up in her clothes, which are huge on me. And he wants me to fix my hair like hers. You know, that big '80s style. You can bet I told him no."

Before Daisy could say no, Brandi refilled her glass. More rum actually sounded like a good idea, but she set the glass down on the countertop. "I shouldn't have more. I haven't eaten."

"Come on. Drink up." Brandi smirked. "What can you tell me about the dead girl Slade was talking to? Do you think they did more than talk? Was she prettier than me?"

"Rene Williams was short, brunette and healthy. I don't think she and Slade did anything more than talk. She'd just broken up with her live-in boyfriend." Daisy wondered if the feds had interrogated Josh Santana. "Is Slade the kind of guy who plays around?"

"He seems shy, but I'm not so sure."

Daisy sipped her rum. "Does he often take off on trips by himself?"

"No more than any other guy. He goes hunting and fishing." Her gaze sharpened as she confronted Daisy, then she slipped back into her vlogging personality and rolled her eyes. "You can't possibly think he's killing off women in his spare time."

When Daisy shook her head, she could feel her

brain rattling inside her skull—an effect of the liquor. "This serial killer likes to stalk his prey."

"Damn, that's creepy. And it's not Slade. My honey-boo is a lot of things, but subtle isn't one of them."

Daisy wondered if she'd said too much. She lacked the finesse to direct this conversation with Brandi. "Are you playing me?"

"That's how I earn a living. I influence plain girls, make them think that if they use a certain brand of mascara, their eyes will shine. If they use my lipstick, their thin lips will look full and lush like mine."

"You lie to them."

"And I get paid for it." She preened. "Listen to me, sugar buns. You're wasting your time talking to my boo."

Daisy felt the same way. She liked Slade. But didn't the people who met Ted Bundy say the same thing about him? *Such a nice young man.*

Chapter Eleven

Still staring at the photo, Carter listened to Slade's monolog about Mama, who was obviously the love of his life. She came from Philly, where her family owned several clothing stores. They'd made sure Elizabeth was well provided for, financing her lifestyle with a trust fund.

Her son thought she'd been happy and had fallen in love with the West. After his dad deserted them, Elizabeth refused to go back east. She got involved with several charities in Pueblo, supported the ballet and the art museum.

"She was a wonderful person." Slade's eyes gleamed with unshed tears.

"Never remarried?"

"She said I was the only man she needed in her life. Sweet, huh?"

"Yeah. Sweet." But Carter couldn't help cringing. It sounded like Mama had developed a fairly unhealthy relationship with her young son.

"She promised she'd never leave me and made me say the same words back to her."

A very unhealthy relationship. "Does Brandi remind you of her?"

"Heck, yes. They're both opinionated ladies. And they don't mind telling me what to do."

He often spoke of his mother in the present

tense. Carter had a feeling that no other woman would ever measure up to Mama. Time to change the topic. "I have a couple of questions about your work schedule, starting with location. Do you always work in Pueblo?"

"No, sir, I go all over the state. Mostly in southwestern Colorado."

"Have you ever worked in Glenwood Springs?" Carter held his breath. If Slade has been in Glenwood on June 10, when Hannah was killed, he'd jump to the top of the suspect list. "Maybe earlier this month?"

"Not in June. Last time I was there, it had just snowed. I think it was April."

"Do you keep a record of your jobs?"

"You bet I do. Come with me to my office, and we can check it out."

In the dining room, Slade paused to play opening from "Moonlight Sonata" on the upright piano—a haunting melody that stuck with Carter as he followed the man into a hallway that bisected the house. At the end closest to the street was a bedroom. Carter took a backward step to glimpse the nondescript furniture with double beds and blah curtains. Probably a guest room. Next to that was a bathroom, which had obviously been renovated, probably enlarged. The cabinetry and fixtures were beautiful and new, reinforcing Brandi's opinion that Slade had talent.

The home office featured a custom-made oak

desk and bookshelves. Across one wall were three-drawer wood file cabinets. Though a computer sat on the desktop, Slade lowered himself into the swivel chair behind the desk, reached into the center drawer and pulled out a ledger. "What did you need to know?" he asked.

"You're very organized."

"Anything worth doing is worth doing well. That's what Mama always says."

His mother might have died two years ago, but Slade hadn't buried her. "I'm surprised you don't use the computer."

"I most certainly do," he said. "It's great for running invoices and keeping track of payments. And I've also got mailing lists. But I like to use the ledger for scheduling. I can scribble in changes or switch things up with sticky notes. The first contractor I worked for used a system like this, and I adopted it for myself."

Carter suspected Slade was a good businessman—likable, skilled and efficient. "Tell me the last time you were in Glenwood Springs. And can I see your schedule for earlier this month?"

"Sure thing."

Carter came around the desk to look over his shoulder. Entries in the ledger were neatly numbered and noted in dark blue pen. From April 21 to April 25, he had installed bookshelves and cabinets in an office and playroom in Glenwood. There were other out-of-town jobs to Durango, near the

Southern Ute Reservation, and at a hunting lodge in Buena Vista. Nothing special had been noted for June 10, when he was in Pueblo for an extended period of time working for a contractor on a development of five new homes.

"When you do the out-of-town jobs," Carter asked, "do you stay in your camper truck?"

"Sometimes, and sometimes I get a motel room. Depends on how tired I am and how cold it is. I've got my camper fixed up real nice with a propane stove and lantern but no extra heat."

"Must be comfortable. You took it to Butcher's Gulch for a mini-vacation."

"I have a platform on one side for a mattress. Underneath are cabinets for my tools."

"What about water?"

"I try to camp near a lake or creek." He closed his ledger. "I've been thinking about buying a trailer or an RV."

"What's stopping you?"

"Brandi would hate that. She doesn't like sleeping outdoors, and don't get me started on how long it takes for her to put on makeup—"

Carter didn't have to wait long for the inevitable comparison. Slade filled in the blank. "—just like Mama."

From outside the office, a burst of feminine laughter erupted. Brandi and Daisy stumbled through the door. Daisy's cheeks flushed a bright red, and he was pretty sure that they hadn't been drinking water in the kitchen. Turning to Brandi, she held her forefinger across her lips in a gesture meant to convey secrecy.

But Brandi wouldn't be stopped. She held up her slender wrist and pointed to an oversize watch. "You've got to go, Slade, if you don't want to be late for your, um, appointment."

He glanced at Carter. "She's right. Are we done here?"

Before he linked arms with Daisy, Carter pulled a business card from his pocket. "I appreciate your time. Give me a call before you leave town." *Or decide to kill again.*

Slade's eyes narrowed. His smile darkened as he said, "You'll be first to know."

Carter recognized the undertone. Slade's comment was a threat.

BACK IN THE SUV, with Carter behind the wheel, Daisy inhaled and exhaled slowly and fought the dizzy sensation caused by whirling rush-hour traffic on their way toward FBI headquarters. *Shouldn't have guzzled that second glass of rum.* Especially not on an empty stomach. Brandi had been conning her, bragging about Slade and how talented and clever he was. Daisy feared she might have blurted something out. "Slade takes off on a lot of hunting and fishing trips where he's out of touch. And he tried to get Brandi to play dress-up in Mama's clothes."

"His issues with Mama are seriously abnormal." He glanced over at her. "Are you okay?"

"I kind of had a glass, or maybe two, of clear rum. Brandi was trying to get me loaded."

"Why?"

"I'm not sure. Maybe so I wouldn't give her boyfriend any trouble." *Inhale and exhale.* "Did you learn anything new from talking to him."

"You might say so."

She squinted her eyes and concentrated hard on his description of the photograph Slade had shown him. When Carter talked about the scarf, a shiver went down her spine. She sobered up quickly, thinking of the first scarf she'd seen on Rene, then the second on Andrea Lindstrom.

In her slightly inebriated condition, Daisy easily imagined monsters—scary ghouls dancing to the repetitive melody of "Moonlight Sonata" plucked out note by note on Slade's upright piano. Her pulse thrummed, but she managed to keep her emotions in check. The important thing to keep in mind—the only thing, really—was the investigation. The brutal murders of these young women had to stop, and it fell to Carter and the FBI and Dr. Julia and all the other law enforcement personnel to follow every lead and apprehend the serial killer. The photograph led Carter to believe he'd found sufficient reason to suspect Slade, but she wasn't so sure.

"You can't be certain of anything," she said.

"How drunk are you? The photo is a solid clue."

"Is it?" she questioned. "Just because his mama wore a scarf doesn't prove that Slade is a psycho murderer."

"Psycho," he said. "That's accurate. Slade reminds me of Tony Perkins in *Psycho*. He looks so innocent until he attacks. Do you remember that movie?"

She avoided horror movies and didn't want to dig into her fears. *Inhale slowly, exhale.* She changed the subject. "What was the name of the cemetery in the photo?"

"Rolling Hills."

"It's a big one, over three hundred acres, just south of Pueblo." She kind of hated that she knew so much about graveyards. "I haven't searched there, because they have a registry with names and the locations of most of the marked graves. Didn't you mention that Hannah came to Pueblo for a funeral? Maybe she bumped into Slade at Rolling Hills. He strikes me as the sort of son who visits Mama's grave often."

"Now you're thinking." He shot her an approving glance. "I'll have Agent Wiley check on where Mama is buried. I'm sure Hannah's great-uncle is at Rolling Hills."

"I wonder whose funeral Slade and Mama were attending."

"He said it was a local church lady. I wrote the name down."

"Are you going to talk to her family?"

"Wouldn't hurt to find out what other people think of Slade and Mama Franklin." He shrugged. "I have a feeling they'll tell me he's a pleasant, hardworking young man who took good care of his mother."

"I'd probably say the same." She liked Slade and his girlfriend. Once she'd gotten past Brandi's brash exterior, she enjoyed talking to the busty brunette who was incredibly proud of her guy in spite of his poor taste in home furnishings. "If he's the murderer, why would he drop such a huge clue? Why show you a photo with a scarf in it?"

"I don't think he realized the implication," Carter said. "His breathing stayed calm and level. His expression didn't change."

"Maybe he's innocent."

"Or maybe he's a split personality, like Dr. Jekyll and Mr. Hyde. One side is a nice, friendly carpenter while the other is a serial killer."

"I know that syndrome exists." She'd studied the neurological anomalies present with dissociative identity disorder, which sometimes resulted from concussion or another brain trauma. As soon as she focused on anatomy, her thinking became less blurry. "The pathology is similar to amnesia. There are examples of individuals with multiple personalities, but it's unusual."

He parked at the curb outside the office building with the FBI headquarters on the eighth floor. "I might mention the Jekyll/Hyde thing if that's what it takes to get a warrant for Slade's camper. When the FBI forensics team processes his truck, they'll find any evidence that exists. Blood or a hair or fiber, something to prove he used his vehicle to transport the victims."

Her suspicions circled back to Eric Wolff and the blue van he used for his house-painting supplies. "Can we also get a warrant for Eric? He admitted to planting a tracking device on me."

"We can try to get a warrant, even though it's a long shot. He can claim you're friends and you gave him permission. Your word against his. Maybe we should pay him a visit while we're in Pueblo."

"Isn't the FBI going to interrogate him?" She enjoyed imagining creepy Eric in handcuffs being led into a little room with a big mirror, even though she didn't think he was a killer. "Shouldn't the feds take him into custody?"

"I get it. You don't like the guy. But that doesn't turn him into a suspect."

"What about this—he showed up at Butcher's Gulch, admitted to stalking me and might have been in Glenwood Springs when Hannah was killed."

"We'll talk to him again. I promise."

Daisy exited Carter's car and stood very still on the sidewalk, allowing her woozy feelings to abate. She gazed toward the mountains west of town. The sun wouldn't dip behind the Sangre de Cristos for a couple more hours, but the light had thinned. Day was almost gone. "We aren't going to have enough time to explore my graveyards today, are we?"

"If we hurry, we can get to one of them before dark." He escorted her through the glass doors into the ground-floor lobby, where they were screened and issued visitor badges from the security guard at the front desk. Carter continued, "I don't know how I'm going to drop you off in Leadville, which is two and a half hours away, and return to pick you up in the morning."

"Well, I have to be here tomorrow. That's non-negotiable." She took an adamant position. "Dr. Julia is going to let me participate in Andrea's autopsy. The exposure to the elements and mauling by animals makes her case even more interesting than Rene's. Doing the autopsies is a tangible way I can be useful."

"Then we've got a problem," he said as he clipped on the visitor's pass. "Too many things to do and not enough time to take care of business."

He was right, and she didn't want to get in the way of the investigation, especially since he seemed to be making progress. "You could take me to my aunt's house and stay over. Then we could leave together early in the morning."

He crossed the air-conditioned lobby and stopped in front of the elevators. "Or you could spend the night with me."

After a momentary burst of panic, she absorbed his suggestion. They both understood the sheer impossibility of a relationship. Nothing serious could develop between them. They were too different. If she spent the night at his house, they had to maintain a distance. *I can do that.*

Daisy wasn't a love-starved maniac like the teenagers she taught in high school. Surely she could keep her hands off the tall, sexy, blue-eyed ranger. "You live in Salida, right?"

"Between Salida, Cañon City and Florence, near the Royal Gorge. My cabin is about an hour away from here."

None of the locations he mentioned rang a bell for her. She tried to visualize a map in her head but didn't know enough to make sense of the twists and turns of the highways and side roads. The towering fourteeners formed an indecipherable, snow-covered mass. Streams, rivers and creeks traversed the landscape. He might as well have told her he lived on the moon. "I'm guessing your cabin is far away from civilization."

"You know me well." They boarded the elevator.

What if he didn't have water or electricity? Of course he did. She was being ridiculous. "Do you have a guest room?"

"Two guest rooms, two bathrooms, a fully stocked kitchen and a state-of-the-art security system to keep intruders at bay. And I have another car you could drive."

She really liked the idea of security and protection. If she agreed to stay there, she needed to make a stop before they left Pueblo to purchase a couple of T-shirts, underwear and a toothbrush. "I'll think about it."

The elevator door swooshed open, and they entered headquarters through an unmarked door. At 5:25, they'd passed quitting time, but the FBI office hummed with activity. The agents who weren't on the phone were tapping away on computer keys. Special Agent in Charge Wiley and red-haired Agent Hicks strode toward them in tandem.

Wiley shook her hand. "Dr. Julia wants me to hire you."

"So do I," Carter whispered.

"I appreciate the compliment, but I already have a job in Denver." Carter wanted her to stay. On some level, Daisy knew what he wanted, and she most definitely didn't intend to discuss the topic right here, right now, in front of Wiley and the other feds. She gestured to the busy room. "What's going on? Do you have a new lead?"

"As soon as news of a serial killer hits the internet and television, we get dozens of leads, most of which are bogus. Nonetheless, we need follow up on each and every call."

"Even that jerk with a sheep ranch and a telescope," Hicks said. "He always reports a UFO landing and aliens killing and/or probing young women."

"Sorry to bring you more work," Carter said. "I'd

like to get warrants to search the vehicles belonging to a couple of legitimate suspects."

Wiley perched on the edge of a vacant desk. "Convince me."

While Carter recounted their conversation with Slade and his girlfriend, she checked out the room. A huge whiteboard listed the victims' names along with their photographs, dates of their murders and locations. Beside it was a map of southwestern Colorado with murder sites highlighted in red marker. Forensic technicians in lab coats drifted among the desks. Most of the agents drank from mugs, and she could only hope they were having soothing herbal tea. Some used land lines, others held cell phones to their ears and a few had headsets. Several scanned their computer screens.

Though she knew the FBI had better forensic resources than state or local branches of law enforcement, the pace and volume of activity impressed her. As SAC, Wiley had his hands full coordinating the operation. Even the muscle-bound Hicks showed himself to be capable of more than flexing as he hammered Carter with intelligent, pointed questions.

Looking around, she recognized the obvious: this investigation centered on real victims and serious consequences. Her petty romantic concerns about staying at Carter's cabin seemed trivial by comparison. To spend the night with Carter or not to spend the night. Was that the question? *Grow up, Daisy.*

She could solve her own dilemma by getting a motel room here in Pueblo and using a rideshare service. Assisting Dr. Julia represented a *real* contribution to the investigation, and Daisy ought to stick to her area of expertise.

At a break in his conversation with Wiley, she pulled Carter aside. In a low voice, she said, "I'm going to stay in town at a motel, but I need to make a stop first and pick up a few things."

"I thought we were going to a graveyard." He actually looked disappointed about not visiting another cemetery. *Seriously?* "Let me at least give you a ride."

"I'll call a rideshare."

"Okay, if that's what you want, but if you change your mind or need help, don't hesitate to call me."

"Why would I need help?"

"No reason. Just offering."

In Denver, she lived alone and took care of herself. Not a problem. After a quick consultation with Agent Hicks, she had the name of a decent motel, where she booked a room. Using a cell phone app, she arranged for a rideshare to pick her up outside the FBI building in nine minutes.

She scanned the room for Carter and saw him staring in her direction. Taller than most of the people around him, he seemed to be above the chaos and furious activity. Calmly, he raked his fingers through his black hair, raised his hand to wave and offered a smile. Such a handsome man, but he looked worried.

For a moment, she remembered Dr. Julia's advice about victimology, especially the part about not taking risks and making sure that someone—like Carter—had her back. Daisy almost reversed her plan before she realized there was no reason to consider herself a target. Sure, Eric was stalking her, but he was after Brighton's Bullion, and she'd made a deal with him to share info. Slade had his hands full with Brandi.

Daisy had nothing to fear.

Or did she?

Chapter Twelve

Outside the FBI building, the rideshare Daisy had contacted arrived precisely on schedule. She gave the driver, Marlene, the address of the motel and settled back. Marlene—a motherly woman with short, frizzy hair and cat-eye sunglasses—drove a spotless Hyundai that smelled of lavender air freshener, reminding her of Slade's mama. When she looked out the window, Daisy spotted a dark blue van on the opposite side of the street and was glad when it pulled away before she had a chance to study the logo. *Not Eric again!* She refused to let him frighten her. The creep lived in Pueblo and might be here by coincidence. *Yeah, right.*

At the pink stucco Sundowner Motel, she asked Marlene to wait for her to check in and if she could then drop her off at a place where she could buy all the everyday stuff she'd left behind when she and Carter drove away from Leadville. After a quick peek into room number eighteen on the second floor—plain, simple and clean, with a small circular table by the window and two full-size beds—she jumped back into the Hyundai. After arranging to return in a half hour, Marlene dropped her off at a superstore where she could purchase everything from deodorant to diamonds. Daisy marched her shopping cart through the automated doors.

Buying toothpaste and T-shirts gave her a pleasant feeling of normalcy. As long as there were superstores, she could put down roots anywhere. She picked up the basics: aspirin, travel-size shampoo, moisturizer and toothbrush. The familiar array of products and the layout of the store lulled her into a sense of security—possibly a false sense. She reminded herself that Andrea Lindstrom had been grabbed in a grocery store parking lot. Shaking her head, she erased the last bit of alcohol-induced relaxation. *Stay alert.*

She headed toward the women's department, where she could pick up a change of clothes. When her cart rounded the end of the aisle, she came face-to-face with a white-haired man, tall and heavyset, hauling an oxygen tank in his cart. He glared at her.

After an aisle dance where they both went left, then right, he muttered, "I know you."

A threat. She backed away, whipping her cart in a U-turn and going to the end of the aisle. The comfortable atmosphere of the store darkened. What had made her think she was safe in here? These customers and clerks could all be serial killers…or worse. *Really?* What was worse? Before she turned into the next aisle, she thought she spotted Eric.

The old man bumped the back of her legs with his cart. Still glaring, his ruddy complexion and broken capillaries primarily on his bulbous nose hinted at alcoholism. He pointed at her and shook his head.

She zipped away from him. Her imagination soared out of control. Why, oh why hadn't she agreed to spend the night at Carter's cabin? Even if she wasn't targeted as a victim, she knew too much about the investigation—enough that the killer might consider her a threat.

But she needed to be able to take care of herself. Dashing through racks of clothes, she grabbed a couple of T-shirts, a pair of cargo pants and a six-pack of socks. Glancing over her shoulder, she saw the old man again.

Before she realized what she was doing, Daisy found herself racing toward the sporting goods section of the store. She approached a clerk behind the counter. "I want to buy a handgun."

"Sorry, miss. We don't handle firearms anymore."

Frantically, she scanned their selection of bows and arrows and all manner of hunting knives. Who was she kidding? Unlike her aunt, a skilled markswoman, Daisy didn't know how to use any kind of lethal weapon. And she had flunked the freebie self-defense class at her gym. Still, she needed a way to protect herself—needed help, someone to back her up. She needed Carter.

Not the most independent thought she'd ever had. But a logical, rational solution. After a quick dash through the grocery section, she hit the checkout line, where she checked her rideshare app. Marlene was out in front, waiting. *Thank God!* Before leaving the store, Daisy armed herself with her pepper spray attached to her key chain.

Outside, she boarded Marlene's bronze Hyundai with her two large shopping bags and her purse. Immediately, she felt mothered and safe. As she shuffled her supplies into a zippered paisley duffel bag she'd bought for easy handling, she said, "Back to the Sundowner."

"Are you okay? You seem unsettled."

"This scary old man was following me."

"Do you want to call the police?"

Did she? Was she overreacting to an imaginary threat? *Calm down.* The interior of the car felt too confined. Inhaling and exhaling deeply, she said, "I'll be okay. Do you mind if I lower the window?"

"No problem."

Daisy buzzed the window all the way down and leaned out. At seven o'clock, the evening rush had slowed, and the orange and purple of sunset streaked the skies. She gazed toward the distant, peaceful mountains. Maybe Carter had the right idea, after all. Living close to nature was far preferable to inhaling exhaust fumes.

The Hyundai braked at a stoplight, and a dark blue van rolled to a stop in the lane beside her. Not just any van—the Wolff House Painting logo on the side featured the familiar pyramid of paint cans—but it wasn't Eric behind the steering wheel. The white-haired man rested his bulky forearm on the edge of the open window. He peered down at her with a cold, ugly sneer distorting his ruddy features.

"Hello, Daisy."

WHEN CARTER'S CELL phone rang, he had to dig through stacks of paperwork to find it. Nothing in the FBI background information he'd compiled on Slade Franklin and his girlfriend justified a search warrant for his home and camper. The couple seemed to lead a simple, law-abiding life, but he also appeared to be one of the last to see Rene alive. If the forensics team could search his truck, they might turn up evidence.

Caller ID on his phone showed Daisy's number, and he answered quickly. "Hey, lady, how's it going?"

"Bad. It's going bad, real bad. You said to call if I needed help, and I do."

Her words spilled out in a rush, faster than a churning whitewater current. "Slow down and tell me where you are."

"No, where are you?"

"Same place you left me. FBI headquarters."

"Good, good, good. I thought you might have left for home. But you haven't. Good. I'll be there in a few minutes. Come downstairs to meet me—please, please. I'm in a bronze Hyundai."

"On my way." He rose from the vacant desk where he'd been sitting and waved to Agent Wiley.

To Daisy, he said, "Stay on the line and tell me what happened."

"You won't believe it. I was stalked at a superstore by a huge, white-haired man. I didn't recognize him, but later he was driving Eric's van."

"Stalked, huh?" Carter caught up to Wiley and whispered, "Daisy found something. She's on her way here."

"Got it," Wiley said.

Carter spoke into his phone. "Eric Wolff's van?"

"I got so confused and scared. I tried to buy a gun."

Not wanting to lose his connection with her, he didn't take the elevator. Instead, he plunged into the stairwell and ran down eight levels. "You got a gun?"

"The store didn't sell guns, and I changed my mind anyway." In spite of the weird conversation, she seemed to be calming down. "Okay, we're pulling up in front of the building. I don't see you."

"Almost there." He charged from the stairwell and paused at the security guard's desk. "I'll be right back."

"Hold on, buddy. It's after seven. I need to buzz you in and out."

"Do it."

Carter went to the glass door and waited until a tiny light on a chrome panel turned from red to green. He thundered onto the wide sidewalk outside the office building. The traffic had thinned, and he easily spotted the Hyundai. When he rushed to open her door, she shoved a paisley duffel into his hands.

Turning to the driver, she said, "Thank you, Marlene. You'll get a big tip from me."

"Almost being in a chase with that van was kind of exciting." She craned her head out the window. "Is this really the FBI office?"

"Eighth floor," she said.

Carter set down the duffel, took her arms and turned her toward him. His gaze locked onto her face. "What the hell happened?"

When she looked up at him, he saw the fear in her eyes. Her grip on self-control had dwindled, but she insisted, "I'm fine."

"Don't start this with me, not again." He didn't want to be brushed off with a "fine" when she was upset. "Tell me the truth. I won't think less of you for being scared."

"I'll think less of myself." She placed her palms on his chest, keeping a distance between them while maintaining contact at the same time. "When I hear these horror stories about murderers and feel threatened by things I can't understand or explain, I panic."

He took both her hands and guided them up around his neck. "Start at the beginning and tell me everything."

"I can't." She trembled against him. "We've got to get off the street. I don't want him to see us."

He should have realized that standing in the open on a sidewalk wasn't going to make her feel safe. Usually, he was great at handling people who were frightened, whether a troop of scouts who thought they saw a bear or a hunter who'd shot himself in the foot. Carter always knew what to do, what to say, how to make it all better. But when it came to Daisy, his natural instincts malfunctioned. Clumsily, he took her paisley duffel in one hand and wrapped his other arm around her waist. And here was another problem. He needed a third hand to signal the security guard to unlock the door.

Together, they jogged toward the entrance. If need be, he'd bust through the glass door to get her to safety. Fortunately, that drama was uncalled for. Agent Wiley must have anticipated trouble. He stood waiting to usher them into the building.

As soon as she came inside, Daisy scooted away from the windows and pulled him toward the elevators, where solid walls would hide them from those passing by on the street. Finally, she dived into his embrace and held on so tightly that he felt her heartbeat hammering against his chest.

Carter looked over her head toward Wiley and said, "She was being stalked by a white-haired giant and tried to buy a gun."

Daisy laughed—a sound more wonderful to him than music. But when she tilted back in his arms and looked up, he saw tears streaking down her cheeks. Her smile quivered on her lips. "That's not the whole story."

"Do you want to sit down?" Wiley asked.

"I want to go upstairs," she said, "and file a report so you can arrest that creep."

"Sure thing," Wiley said hesitantly as he adjusted his bolo tie. "And which creep is that?"

"Eric Wolff's father."

Carter nodded. *Not surprised.* Of all the potential suspects he'd researched, Gerald Wolff had the longest criminal record, ranging from dozens of speeding tickets to an assault and battery charge that resulted in a six-month jail sentence. For most of his life, the sixty-three-year-old man had worked a good-paying job at the steel mill. He'd been divorced for fifteen years. While he was married, his ex-wife had filed four restraining orders against him.

Now, it seemed, old Gerald had been stalking Daisy. Just like his son, Eric. The rotten apple didn't fall far from the tree.

Chapter Thirteen

On the eighth floor in an FBI conference room, Daisy took the chair at the head of an eight-foot-long table and dug into her paisley duffel for the burritos, guac and chips she'd snagged at the superstore. Carter sat on her right, facing the windows where a brilliant sunset devoured the mountains. On her left was SAC Wiley and Agent Hicks, who activated a recording device so they wouldn't lose a single word of her narrative.

Even before she spoke, she began to feel foolish about her panic. An old man had accosted her. So what? The whole thing was totally unimportant—unless Gerald Wolff turned out to be the serial killer. "I might be overreacting."

"Mr. Wolff doesn't fit the standard serial killer profile," Agent Hicks said. "Typically, they're white males between twenty-eight and forty-five. Gerald is sixty-three."

"I guess that means Jackknife Jones is also eliminated."

"Not so fast." Wiley flipped through his file folder and found a photo of Jones that actually didn't look too bad. With his scraggly hair pulled back in a neat man bun and his chin shaved, he appeared younger. "He's on the older side. But only fifty-two."

"I would have guessed twenty years older," Daisy said. "I guess he's lived a hard life."

"You're giving him the benefit of the doubt," Wiley said. "He's made his own life choices, some of which have landed him in jail. Usually on charges of petty theft."

"I really don't like having him sniff around my aunt Vi."

"Don't blame you," Wiley said.

Daisy poked at her burritos with a plastic fork. Food had seemed like a good idea, but she couldn't imagine putting anything into her churning stomach. After one small bite, her stomach groaned. Nope, nothing to eat or drink, not right now.

SAC Wiley encouraged her to get started with her narrative. "From the beginning, right after you checked in at the motel."

"After I peeked into my room, I asked my rideshare driver, Marlene, to take me shopping. She dropped me off at one of those stores that have groceries and everything else. Except for guns—I couldn't buy a handgun."

Wiley raised an eyebrow. "You're jumping ahead, Daisy. Let's go in sequence. What did you purchase first?"

She described her foray through cosmetics and her aisle dance with Gerald Wolff. "At the time, I didn't know who he was. I've never actually met the man, but he visited my aunt Vi in Leadville. Gerald and Eric think they have a claim on Brighton's Bullion because their ancestor Morris Wolff was part of Sherwood Brighton's outlaw gang."

"But you don't agree," Wiley said.

"Saying that he has as much right to the fortune as Aunt Vi is ridiculous. Sherwood was the leader of the pack and Morris was an underling. Plus he might have been having an affair with Sherwood's wife."

"Maybe Sherwood wanted to cut him out," Wiley said. "For revenge."

"Doubtful. Sherwood left records of how he planned and executed the robberies. Morris Wolff was hardly mentioned. He definitely wasn't a partner. Even if he was, even if the treasure actually exists, we've made a deal with Eric to give him a share."

Agent Hicks folded his arms and flexed his biceps. "It exists. There are lots of people who believe in the bullion."

"Which doesn't make it real," she said. "In any case, the treasure isn't connected to the serial killer. Or is it?"

The three men exchanged a look before Carter spoke up. "We can't ignore the coincidence, Daisy. If we take Eric seriously as a suspect, there might be a link."

"Let's leave that topic for later," Wiley said. "Please continue."

She ran through the rest of her narrative, taking the story to the point when Gerald peered down at her from the van and said hello. Her lips pinched together. She'd never forget the sound of his rough-edged voice—a growl that sounded like he had a mouthful of broken glass. "He threatened me."

Carter reached over and placed his large hand on top of hers. "Keep going, Daisy. You're doing great. What did he say?"

"He told me not to think I was so smart. If me and my aunt—he called her a bitch—didn't find his treasure soon, we'd be sorry."

Wiley prompted, "Did he say how you'd be sorry?"

"He didn't have a chance," she said. "I stuck my arm out of the car window and blasted my pepper spray at him."

Her action had been unplanned. Pure instinct. Scared, she'd struck out blindly. Didn't know if she hit him before she frantically buzzed the window up and yelled at Marlene to drive fast. Get away from the blue van. Go to the FBI building.

Remembering, her pulse beat as fast as a snare drum. In spite of the office air-conditioning, sweat moistened her forehead and back. She turned her hand palm up and laced her fingers with Carter's, needing his steady, calm strength to anchor herself. "And then," she concluded, "I called Carter and came here."

Hicks asked, "Anything else you can recall about the old man? Did he have a weapon? In the store, did he touch you?"

"He bumped me with his shopping cart." She glanced back and forth between Carter and the two FBI agents. What was going on here? Didn't they believe her? "He should be in jail."

SAC Wiley said, "His actions don't rise to the level of assault. We can't arrest a man for shopping. Or for saying hello."

Slowly, she stood. Her hands balled into fists at her side, ready to fight. "He called my aunt Violet a bitch and told me we'd be sorry if we didn't find his gold."

"I wish there was something we could do," Wiley said.

For most of her life, she'd been polite and controlled. She longed to throw caution to the wind, to scream her head off and color outside the lines. Why should she allow Gerald Wolff to menace her? Whirling, she pointed to the door of the conference room. "Out there, you've got a gang of agents following up on improbable leads from every weirdo in the state of Colorado. Why not the Wolff men—father and son?"

"We need evidence," Hicks said.

"They both stalked me. Their blue van appeared at the crime scene in Butcher's Gulch. And maybe they were in Glenwood."

"We don't know for sure if the timing matched Hannah's murder," Hicks said. "And she described the man she was meeting to visit Doc Holliday's grave as being younger."

"It could have been Eric. Father and son could be working together," Daisy said. "That's possible, isn't it? A serial killer team?"

Carter got up and stood beside her. "I agree with Daisy. We can't let Wolff threaten her and walk away. I'll go to his house and interrogate him."

Her heart swelled with pride and gratitude as she took a step toward him. Carter believed in her. He stood up for her.

"Whoa there, Ranger." Hicks slammed his fist on the table. "The FBI has jurisdiction on this investigation."

"Thanks for the reminder." Carter confronted him. "I don't answer to you guys. I work for NPS."

"Shoes," Daisy said emphatically. "You've got footprints from the murder scenes, and Gerald Wolfe is a big man—probably size thirteen."

"That could be evidence," SAC Wiley said. "Maybe enough for a search warrant."

"Yes." She did a fist pump.

"Big feet aren't a crime, but we'll interrogate. Carter, you shouldn't approach him, because he already knows you're allied with Daisy. Hicks and I will talk to him."

"When?" Carter asked.

"Right after dinner." Wiley's forehead pinched in a scowl. "My wife made me promise to watch my diet. If I don't eat healthy food on a regular basis, I get cranky."

"The crankier, the better," Daisy said. "I want you to scare that old man."

"It's time for the two of you to go home until tomorrow," he said. "Hicks and I will use an open channel on a transmitter so you can both listen in on our interrogation."

Satisfied with the compromise, Daisy headed toward the door. Over her shoulder, she said, "Help yourselves to the burritos and guac. I'm not hungry."

Marching away from the FBI headquarters, she felt equal measures of bravery and silliness. Was she acting on the facts? Or had she gotten swept away by her own panic? Either way, she was happy about two things. Number one: Gerald Wolff wasn't going to get away with scaring her. Number two: Carter was on her side.

AT ROOM NUMBER eighteen on the second floor of the Sundowner Motel, Carter paused to scan the asphalt parking lot and traffic on the street below. Not sensing a threat, he entered behind Daisy. Inside, he noted the two full-size beds. If he needed to spend the night at the motel, no problem. Of course, he'd rather take Daisy home to his cabin, where she could feel safe and he could relax and maybe, just maybe, take their relationship to a more intimate level. Their kiss this morning deserved a follow-up, and he was ready, especially when she kicked off her hiking boots and stretched out on the bed closest the door. Her well-toned, golden-tan legs almost reached the end of the mattress. She flexed her foot and wiggled her toes. Typically, he didn't have a foot fetish, but she was enough to make him change his mind.

Before he started drooling, he shifted his focus to the takeout dinner from the Happy Dragon—three large bags with veggie fried rice, chow mein, ginger beef, egg rolls, sweet and sour pork, kung pao chicken, cheese wontons, and fortune cookies. Had he overordered? Oh, yeah, he was starving. He'd also picked up a six-pack of bottled water. Before he settled down to eat, he set up the transmitter on the dresser by the television so they could hear the team of Wiley and Hicks interrogate Gerald Wolff.

Daisy rolled onto her stomach and exhaled a sound that was halfway between a groan and a giggle. "I've never had a day like this," she said. "Best of times and worst of times."

"Yeah? What was the best?" In his mind, he replayed their kiss by Teacup Lake.

"The autopsy, of course."

He should have guessed. "And the worst?"

"Being scared by the big bad Wolff."

He appreciated her sense of humor but knew she used jokes to deflect her real feelings. This woman didn't like being vulnerable. "I'm sorry that happened to you."

"Not your fault."

"I know. But if I'd been with you, Wolff never would have come close."

"True. You're definitely an alpha male."

"Can we be serious for a minute?" He stood and went to the transmitter, tuning the sensitive radio to the channel Wiley would use. "I'd feel better if I could—with your permission—keep an eye on you."

"Like a bodyguard?"

Exactly like a bodyguard. "I want to be sure you're safe."

For a long moment, she considered. No doubt weighing the positive of having protection against the negative of being watched over by a babysitter. She solemnly nodded. "Okay."

While he called Wiley and made sure they were properly connected, she spread food cartons on the small table by the window. Chopsticks in hand, they dug in. According to Brandi's influencer vlog, Happy Dragon ranked in the top five Chinese take-out places in Pueblo. Admittedly not a huge selection, but he was so hungry that he could have eaten a huge platter of Rocky Mountain oysters. At first, Daisy picked at her food, but her enthusiasm grew as she tasted the spicier dishes.

He enjoyed watching her balance large chunks of ginger beef on the tip of her chopsticks, then dab at her mouth with dainty touches. He grinned. "In your expert opinion, what's the best Asian food in Denver?"

She rattled off three different places without thinking twice. "And I love dim sum on Sunday morning, especially sticky rice and pot stickers. What about you? Cops are supposed to know the best places to eat."

"I agree with your picks." His worry that they didn't have a single thing in common vanished. Apparently, they were both foodies. "I took a class in how to make sushi."

"You've got to show me." She gestured with her chopsticks. "But how do you get good, fresh fish in the mountains?"

"Not fresh," he admitted. "We've got no ocean. But we do have refrigeration."

The transmitter on the dresser buzzed to life, and Carter went to turn up the volume.

He heard Wiley's deep, authoritative voice. "FBI. Open the door, Mr. Wolff."

Words to strike terror in the heart of a guilty person.

Chapter Fourteen

Daisy dropped her chopsticks and stared at the transmitter, amazed at the clarity of the audio. Introductions between Gerald Wolff and the FBI agents sounded like they were standing across the room instead of being miles away. Carter returned to his seat at the small table, reached over and gave her hand a gentle squeeze.

She squeezed back. "I'm glad we're not there."

"I wish we were."

A perfect illustration of the differences between them. She preferred to observe the situation from a safe distance—clinically noting facts and discrepancies—while Carter was a man of action.

From her prior encounter with Gerald, she had deduced probable alcoholism. In this conversation, he was huffing and coughing like a man with advanced emphysema. His tone was hostile. "What the hell do you feds want?"

"We're investigating the murders of two women," Wiley said. "Is your son at home?"

"Eric ain't here. And we got nothing to do with murder."

"Your dark blue van was sighted near the crime scene. Eric admitted being there. Were you with him?"

"Hell, no." He gasped and grumbled. "I hardly

ever use the van. Supposedly, Eric is running things. Running his business into the ground, if you ask me."

"You worked at the steel mill," Wiley said, "but you're retired."

"The bastards made me retire early because of my disability. Can't stand on my feet all day so I don't get my full pension. I'm only sixty-three, you know."

Agent Hicks spoke up. "Do you own another vehicle?"

"None of your damn business."

"You met Ms. Brighton today," Wiley said.

"So that's why you're paying me a visit. Well, good. The little bitch attacked me. You can lock her up. Take a look at my arm. She blasted me with pepper spray."

Under her breath, Daisy said, "And I'm glad I did. I hope it hurts."

Wiley ignored Gerald's complaint. "You were stalking Ms. Brighton."

"You can't prove it. We just happened to be in the same store at the same time." She heard him grunt, probably while shifting his bulk in a chair. "Little Miss Daisy and her auntie are trying to take my bullion, my inheritance."

Wiley continued. "Eric admitted that he put a tracker on Ms. Brighton."

"A game between the two of them. Nothing but a prank. No harm done."

"I've advised her to register for a restraining order. I believe your ex-wife filed several such orders against you."

"Don't care what she did. I'm glad the ugly old sow is out of my life."

"You had domestic violence arrests, but your wife dropped the charges. Do you have a problem with women, Mr. Wolff?"

Daisy could only guess at the depth of his awfulness. His behavior—the cruelty and the rage—fit her expectations of a serial killer who lashed out at women, cut their throats and watched them bleed to death. But the behavior of this particular killer also included tenderness. He cared for his victims and tied pretty silk scarves around their throats.

Wiley switched the topic to Eric, probing to discover how he'd felt after his mother left. Did he blame his father for chasing her away? Not according to Gerald, who stated that he'd done a great job of raising his teenaged son by himself, didn't put up with whining and used a firm hand to show the kid what was expected of him.

"I taught that long-haired punk everything he knows." Gerald lapsed into a bout of coughing. "Showed him how to paint houses and how to bargain with his suppliers. And I taught him how to handle the ladies. You know what I mean?"

Wiley asked, "Did you also teach Eric how to stalk a woman?"

"When you want something," Gerald said, "you

have to go after it. You've got to study your prey, see where she goes and what she likes. Then you make your move. And you take what you want from her."

"What if she doesn't want to give it up?"

"They always do," Gerald said.

Daisy groaned. *Disgusting!*

In SAC Wiley's voice, she heard barely suppressed rage. "Is Eric stalking Daisy because he wants to make her his woman?"

"Could be. She's not bad-looking."

"Does he have other girlfriends?"

"What are you getting at?" Wolff growled.

"Does the name Rene Williams mean anything to you? How about Hannah Guerrero?"

"I don't know them."

"Was it your son or was it you, Gerald? Are you the Wolff who got too close to these ladies? Eileen Findlay. Andrea Lindstrom."

She heard the ring of steel in Wiley's voice as he listed the victims. With his thinning hair and his bolo tie, Wiley might not look like a hardened federal officer, but—according to Carter—he had one of the highest arrest records in the Rocky Mountain West.

Over the transmitter, she heard a door open. A new voice joined the others. Eric Wolff had come home. "Good evening, gentlemen. What's going on here?"

"Back off!" the older Wolff roared at his son. "I can take care of myself."

"Don't you get it, Dad? They're trying to pin the serial murders on you."

"Or you, sonny boy."

"Shut up," Eric snarled.

"Don't you dare backtalk me."

She heard confused muttering and the sounds of a scuffle. Chair legs scraped on the floor. Feet stomped. There was a loud slap. The crash of something breaking. Nervous, she looked to Carter. "What's going on?"

"Some kind of fight." He paced to the dresser where the transmitter stood. Bracing his arms on either side, he looked like he wanted to dive through the radio and join in the brawl. "Wish I knew who was involved."

"Why?"

"I'd like to see Hicks use Gerald's big, fat face for a punching bag. I don't like that guy."

Another crash. She heard Wiley take control. "If you hit him again, you're under arrest."

"He's my son," Gerald said. "If Eric needs discipline, that's my job."

"It's all right," Eric said. "I'm okay."

"You're bleeding," Wiley said. "Do you need medical treatment?"

"It's just a bloody nose. I had it coming." He cleared his throat. "Are we done?"

"What size shoe do you wear?" Agent Hicks asked.

"I'm a twelve. My dad is a thirteen."

"We'll need to take a look in your closet."

Gerald refused loudly while he coughed and huffed. Eric claimed it wasn't any good to talk to him when he was like this. After five minutes' argument, the FBI agents left. Before Wiley ended the transmission, he told Carter that he'd see him tomorrow. His last words: "We'll have a warrant to search their truck, their house and anywhere else you like."

"We win," Carter said as he turned off the transmitter.

In a dull voice, she said, "Yippee."

Daisy pushed away from the small table by the closed motel drapes. Being involved in the investigation had taken her appetite away. She cracked open her fortune cookie and read the scrap of paper inside to herself. *You will find true happiness with a tall, dark, handsome partner.*

She gazed across the table. There sat Carter—Mr. Tall, Dark and Handsome himself. Having him close did a lot to relieve her fears. She pointed at his fortune cookie. "Let's hear your future."

"Sure." He cracked it open and read out loud. "'A beautiful woman will spend the night at my cabin.'"

She grabbed for the fortune, but he pulled it away. "It doesn't say that."

He shrugged. "My real fortune says something about taking a trip over high mountains, which is kind of my job. Accurate but no surprise."

She rolled the idea of spending the night with him around in her mind, then pushed it away. Life was already too complicated. "What did you think about the interrogation?"

"SAC Wiley is a sharp guy, and Gerald is a misogynist who probably abused young Eric."

She sipped water from one of the plastic bottles. "Do those traits fit the profile for a serial killer?"

"I'm afraid so." Carter dug more deeply into the container of veggie fried rice. "Hating women is a biggie. Also, he admitted being a stalker, which suits our killer. Both Hannah and Andrea felt like they were being watched. Abusers sometimes graduate to murder. My boss, Joaquin, would say that Gerald is a narcissist who thinks he's smarter than everybody, especially the feds."

Once again, her imagination cranked into high gear as she thought of the victims seeing the big, ugly face of Gerald Wolff before they died. Instead of a celestial chorus, they'd hear his labored breathing. Something about that picture didn't fit.

She left the table and sat on the bed. "I'm leaning more toward Eric as the killer. He was abused in childhood and lost his mother in his teens. We need to find out more about her. She left him fifteen years ago. Why is he compelled to start killing now?"

He bit into a cream cheese–stuffed wonton. "Abuse is not an excuse."

"What?"

"Just saying." He studied the wonton as though the answers were hidden in the deep-fried folds. "Criminal behavior can't always be blamed on the rotten parents."

She sensed there was something more to his statement but didn't want to go deeper right now. Taking out her cell phone, she said, "It's after nine. I'd better call Vi to let her know I won't be returning to Leadville tonight."

Actually, Daisy was more worried about her aunt than the other way around. Her aunt had been in contact with two of the suspects: Jackknife and Gerald Wolff. She might make an enticing target.

After Daisy explained that she was staying at a motel in Pueblo to save driving time, she asked, "Aunt Vi, has Jackknife been in contact with you?"

"As a matter of fact, he's sitting in the front parlor as we speak."

Warning bells clanged inside her head. "Tell him to go home. Right now."

"I'm never rude to my guests. Besides, I want to reward him for making an effort before he came calling. His hair is combed, he shaved and he must have purchased a clean shirt."

Daisy remembered the photo in the FBI file that showed Jackknife in a more positive light. Still not completely presentable but better than usual.

"Don't encourage him. He's a suspect in the serial killings."

"My dear girl, are you worried about me? There's really no need. I'm carrying my tiny Glock 42 in the pocket of my skirt."

Her blonde, green-eyed, sixty-eight-year-old aunt wasn't a woman who would crumble under threats. "Are you always armed?"

"Frequently. I have a concealed carry permit, after all." She cleared her throat. "Actually, I'm more concerned about you doing autopsies and interrogating criminals. Is that nice forest ranger with you?"

"Yes." She glanced across the room to the table where Carter was tidying up the cartons of Chinese food. *My tall, dark, handsome partner.* "He's not spending the night, though."

"Why not?"

"I haven't known the man for even two days. It's too soon."

"Of course, I agree," aunt Vi said. "But spending the night doesn't necessarily mean you're in the same bed. He could watch over you...like a bodyguard."

Frankly, she didn't trust herself to be alone with Carter and not make a move on him. When she caught him staring at her bare legs, her response was to inch her skirt up even higher. *Time to change into those baggy cargo pants.* Picking up her paisley duffel, Daisy scooted into the bathroom and closed the door. She turned up the water in the sink full blast so Carter couldn't hear her end of the conversation. Still, she whispered, "He invited me to his cabin outside Salida, about an hour away from here."

"Do it," Vi said. "Otherwise, you'll spend the whole night hiding under the covers and listening for the lead-footed approach of Gerald Wolff or Jackknife or any of the other suspects you've been confronting. I remember what you were like as a child."

Daisy wasn't sure what she was talking about. "Can you give me some details?"

"Your parents, especially my sister, are ridiculously overprotective. I was always the wild one, and she was a frightened little mouse. In any case, she wouldn't allow you to watch or listen to anything scary. *Grimm's Fairy Tales* were too violent for her darling Daisy. When you finally had the chance to see a scary movie at a sleepover, you were traumatized. Weeping all night. Screaming at every shadow. Once, when I was babysitting, I found you hiding in your bedroom closet with a butcher knife from the kitchen."

That bit of family background explained a lot. "I really don't remember."

"But you still get scared, don't you?" Aunt Vi's voice had an *I told you so* tone. "I saw that fear when you were talking to Eric. Right this minute, you should march up to Ranger Carter and tell him you're taking him up on his invitation. Do you want me to talk to him? You know, to let him know that you're not agreeing to a night of hanky-panky."

Oh. My. God. "Absolutely not."

"What about his boss? Somebody at the Salida headquarters, maybe."

"No phone calls, Aunt Vi. And you need to get rid of Jackknife. Whatever else you do, no more contact with Gerald or Eric Wolff."

Daisy emerged from the bathroom and shuffled toward Carter in her slightly too large cargo pants that dragged on the maroon-and-gray-patterned carpet. When she reached the table, she set down her cell phone and gazed up into Carter's blue eyes. Before she became mesmerized by the reflection of light in the facets of his irises or the way his black hair fell across his forehead or his incredibly sexy mouth, she spoke up. "I want to stay at your cabin tonight."

"I can make that happen."

Immediately, her imagination settled down. She felt safe.

Chapter Fifteen

Before Carter turned onto the red gravel driveway that led to the detached garage outside his cabin, he killed the headlights on his SUV. Parked behind a stand of leafy green aspen that hid his vehicle from the road, he drew his Beretta from the holster he'd stashed in the locked center console and adjusted the overhead light so it wouldn't flash on when he opened the door.

Daisy roused herself from sleep. In a groggy voice, she asked, "What's going on?"

"Probably nothing." She'd sunk into a heavy nap as soon as they left the lights of Pueblo, and he hadn't wakened her when he noticed headlights following them. "Stay here, and keep the doors locked."

Earlier, when he drove by the NPS headquarters in Salida, he had considered stopping and recruiting Joaquin for backup, but the office was dark. Though it was only a few minutes past ten o'clock, his boss—an early riser—might have already gone to bed at his house on the outskirts of town. Carter didn't want to disturb him for a threat that might not even be real. The headlights in his rearview mirror had disappeared right after he passed the Salida City Limits sign.

He'd contacted SAC Wiley. In a quiet phone conversation, Carter learned that the FBI had placed Gerald Wolff under surveillance—an extreme measure, but suspected serial killers got extreme attention. The dark blue house-painting van hadn't moved, which meant the vehicle stalking his SUV wasn't Wolff. Unless Gerald or Eric had sneaked out and used a different vehicle.

Carter wondered if he was turning paranoid. Never before had unfounded fear been an issue, but Daisy's imagination had infected him like a virus. He felt her panic and saw danger in every shadow. The vehicle following them hadn't come close enough for him to identify the make or model. Then, he didn't see the headlights anymore. Not until he drove on the twisting route leading to his cabin. The stalker was back.

Outside the garage, Carter slipped through the driver's-side door into the night, holding his Beretta at the ready. The waning moon and a cloudless sky full of stars shed enough light to see the edge of the wide driveway, where the adobe-colored gravel spread into thick shrubs and sage. The triple-size wood-frame garage with a shake shingle roof that matched the cabin loomed in front of his SUV. An ancient Jeep with a snowplow attachment on the front was parked under the eaves. On the near side, a rustic path with a sturdy banister led to the covered porch that stretched across the front of his log cabin. None of the interior lights were on, but the stars and moon reflected on the triple-pane glass on the lower floor windows and the twin dormers.

Pacing carefully at the edge of the driveway, Carter made very little noise. A rush of fresh wind slapped him in the face. The smell of forest and arid dust chased away the drowsiness that came from sitting too long in the car. Alert, he was ready to kick butt if necessary and almost hoped one of the suspects had been stupid enough follow them here.

If he'd been alone, he might have darted through the surrounding forest until he located the stalker. He would have turned the tables on this creep. But not tonight, not while Daisy was nearby. His job, his main purpose until they apprehended the serial killer, revolved around her safety. After all, she wouldn't be in this predicament if he hadn't escorted her to Rene Williams's body in the Butcher's Gulch graveyard. Her involvement wasn't all his fault, but Carter deserved a measure of the blame.

Looking over his shoulder toward the car, he tried to see her shadowy silhouette in the front seat, but the night was too dark and the windows too opaque. Without visual verification of her whereabouts, he could only hope she'd followed his instructions and stayed put.

He crouched behind the row of four mailboxes at the edge of his property and watched the road. For a full ten minutes, he held himself motionless.

From years of hunting, he knew how to blend into the forest and wait patiently.

Finally, Carter stood and walked to the center of the two-lane graded gravel road that passed his cabin and curled up the hill toward other properties. He saw no evidence of the other vehicle. Safe to assume he'd given up? Or was he biding his time until later tonight?

He jogged back to the SUV, clicked the locks and opened the passenger-side door. Immediately, he was hit by the smell of deep-fried wontons and spicy ginger seasoning. Daisy held one of the Chinese food containers and a pair of chopsticks.

She grinned. "Are we okay?"

"As far as I can tell." The shift in her mood from near panic to cheerful munching surprised him. Paranoid or not, the lady was unpredictable. "I'll feel safer when we get inside the cabin so I can set the alarms."

"Aye, aye." She saluted with the flick of a chopstick.

Juggling her paisley duffel, the remains of their Chinese dinner and his Beretta, he hiked up the inclined path to the covered porch, tapped a code into the security keypad, listened for the click and swung open the front door. Three years ago, when he had firmly established his assignment as an investigator for the NPS, he'd bought this two-story log cabin with dark green trim and a gray roof. He liked the views and didn't mind the need for repairs. His first improvements included upgraded locks, reinforced windows and an electronic security system designed to protect his home when long assignments kept him from returning. Next, he added the huge garage that also served as a storage area for his ATV and sports equipment. This year, his main project for the summer would be expanding his cedar deck and adding a barbecue.

After he reset the alarm, he watched Daisy stroll around his living room with the rustic stone fireplace and heavy furniture. Her too-long cargo pants lacked the charm of her short skirt, but he liked the way they outlined her firm little bottom. She passed through the dining area, which was dominated by a table he meant to refinish one of these days, and ended her tour in the large kitchen, also partially renovated, with a long, black granite–topped island opposite the dated avocado-green appliances. Her smile seemed forced. “Great place. So much potential.”

“It’s not perfect,” he readily conceded. “My cabin is a work in progress.”

“Too bad Slade Franklin is a suspect. You could use a skilled carpenter who specializes in renovation work.”

“I can’t believe you’d consider hiring a possible serial killer as a handyman.” He unloaded the Chinese food into his fridge. “I get a kick out of working on the house. Some ranger buddies will come over and we’ll make a day of it.”

"Did you ever think you could maybe use a woman's touch?"

"Are you volunteering for the job?"

"No way."

Her answer came too quickly, and she emphasized by waving her hands and taking a couple of backward steps. Apparently, Daisy wanted him to know, for sure, that she wasn't pressing for a deeper relationship, which made him contrary. Now, he wanted her to...want him. "Are you certain that you don't want to step in and be my interior decorator?"

"One hundred percent," she said. "I'm a condo dweller whose fix-up projects are limited to replacing the plants on my balcony when they die."

He offered her a choice of beverage, and she opted for herbal tea. "Are you hungry?" he asked. "I can zap something in the microwave."

"Not necessary."

After he filled the teakettle and set it on the stove top to boil, he pointed to a tall stool on the opposite side of the island. After she sat, he said, "Before you go to bed, there are a couple of questions we need to answer, starting with this one. Do you believe you're in danger?"

"I don't know," she said. "At times, I'm nervous, almost panicky, but I don't have factual evidence to validate those feelings."

In a sentence, she'd summarized the opposite sides of her personality. Should she follow her instincts? Or allow her knowledge to define her behavior? Both approaches had merit, and he didn't know which to believe.

She continued, "I mean, it doesn't make sense for the killer to come after me. I have no connection to any of the women who were murdered. I live in Denver and don't know their friends or families. We all worked in different arenas. What's his motive?"

"Killers aren't known for being rational." He set the tea to brew in a butterfly-and-flower-patterned teapot left behind by a former girlfriend. "None of the other women were connected, except for Andrea and Hannah in Glenwood Springs. They were friends."

"Fancy teapot," she said dryly.

"I know how to steep." He loaded a tray with the pot, cups, sugar, spoons and creamer. "Let's take this conversation into my office. I want to make notes."

"Charts and graphs." She eagerly rubbed her hands together. "I love that stuff."

Not surprised. He suspected her science classroom was packed with interactive displays, including the periodic table, the Fibonacci sequence, see-through models of human anatomy, plastic skeletons and skulls.

He led her down a hallway, passed the bathroom, and entered the home office with square footage nearly equal to the living room. He placed the tea tray on a coffee table in front of a sturdy brown leather sofa. Opposite the sofa stood a large whiteboard—four feet by six—on a heavy-duty frame that backed up to his desk.

With a dark blue marker, Carter wrote the names of the victims, starting with Eileen Findlay, who was killed on the Riverwalk in Pueblo, then Hannah and Andrea. Finally, Rene. "What else would you add?"

With a green marker, she filled in the blanks with each woman's age, occupation, home address and the places where their bodies were found. In front of their names, she wrote the date they were murdered. Stepping back, she regarded the whiteboard and gave a satisfied nod. "I like being organized. On the opposite side of the board we can jot down the suspects."

"Not all of them."

"There aren't that many."

"We don't have access to the complete list," he said. "There are a number of suspicious characters who the FBI keeps under routine surveillance. These are men with criminal records. Some are stalkers. Others have been arrested for harassment or other violence. Bad guys."

He circled the coffee table and poured himself a cup of green chamomile tea, to which he added two teaspoons of raw sugar. After taking a sip, he lowered himself onto the left end of the sofa, his favorite spot, and turned on a brass table lamp. "Our investigation," he said, "is limited to the

Wolff men, father and son, Slade Franklin, and Jackknife Jones."

On the other half of the whiteboard, she listed the names. "Not Rene's boyfriend?"

"The FBI in Denver is keeping an eye on him."

While he watched, she filled in pertinent information about their suspects, including age, address and occupation. He was happy to leave the charting to her and wanted to believe being organized would make a difference.

"I'm glad we're doing this," she said.

"I'm going to ask you again," he said. "Are you in danger? Yes or no."

"Yes."

He saw the fear in her green eyes and heard the tremor in her voice. She believed the answer she'd given, even if she couldn't explain why.

And so did he.

DAISY WANTED THESE serial killings to make sense. Staring at the whiteboard, she picked up a pink marker and said, "This is for alibis or lack thereof."

Sipping his tea from a dainty china cup decorated with butterflies, he looked like a cross between a rugged cowboy and a fancy-pants gentleman. "Explain."

She drew a line connecting Eric to both victims found in Butcher's Gulch. "We know he was in the area and could have committed both of these murders."

"Don't forget," Carter said, "Andrea was abducted on the fourteenth in Glenwood Springs, killed on the seventeenth and her body wasn't found until the twentieth. Did Eric hold her captive for three days?"

She groaned. "I don't suppose he has an alibi for the time period."

"He's self-employed. Timing is based on *his* records, which means he could have gone to Glenwood and lied to us about being there."

She scribbled an *E* for Eric and a pink question mark beside Andrea and Hannah. The line to Eileen Findlay slashed directly across the whiteboard. "Because he lives in Pueblo, it's possible that he doesn't have much of an alibi for the woman found in the Riverwalk."

A similar pattern emerged for self-employed Slade Franklin, who had shown the record of his schedule to Carter without any sort of verification.

Stepping back, she studied the chart and shook her head. "We know almost nothing about the whereabouts of Gerald Wolff. Ditto for Jackknife. He could have been in all those places or in none of them."

Carter joined her at the board. In purple, he wrote a note between the victims and the suspects and drew a circle around a single word. "Warrants," he said. "Wiley promised he'd have the necessary paperwork tomorrow. With any luck, that should produce evidence."

She prepared a cup of tea for herself with one spoonful of sugar and a dab of creamer. "After the ace FBI crime-scene team searches Slade's camper truck and the Wolffs' van, we could have proof that one or more of the victims had contact with our suspects. Otherwise, we have a lack of forensics. No witnesses. No cameras in the area. No DNA or prints."

She sat at the opposite end of the leather sofa and tasted her chamomile tea. The warmth, flavor and fruity apple scent relaxed her. After such a long day, she'd expected to be tired, but the nap on the drive here must have refreshed her. She felt wide-awake—disturbingly so. Her busy brain had begun to spin sexy fantasies about her and Carter, and she had to remind herself to shut down her desires before they got started. Aunt Vi had given her good advice. Spending the night together didn't mean they had to be in the same bed.

In her peripheral vision, she watched him pace in front of the whiteboard. With a yellow marker, he wrote another single-word notation and read it aloud. "Motive."

"That's a good one." Her gaze lingered on his wide shoulders and narrow hips. He was too handsome, too perfect. Talking about these other creeps tarnished her thinking. "We know what makes Gerald tick. He hates women."

"And Jackknife?"

"I'd have to say greed. Didn't he agree to drive me in circles for a payoff?"

"That's what he told me the first time we talked at Butcher's Gulch. He said he got the cash from a kid—an unconnected third party—and didn't know who was behind it."

"How much?"

"He wouldn't say. I had the idea that it wasn't much."

She frowned. "And it doesn't explain how he might make money from the other victims?"

"Jackknife isn't a great suspect, and his motive is weak." He shrugged. "Let's move on. We've got mother issues for Slade and Eric."

"Slade has an unhealthy attachment to Mama. And Eric erupted with rage when he talked about how his mom left with the golden retriever." She gazed at him and smiled. "It's ironic—I know quite a bit about our suspects but almost nothing about you."

"Right back at you."

She wanted to fill in those blanks, wanted to have a clear picture about who he was, what he loved and what made him laugh. His favorite movie? Favorite song? "Tell me all about yourself."

Chapter Sixteen

From her position at the end of the long sofa, Daisy concentrated on her chamomile and tried to ignore the magnetic pull that impelled her toward Carter, who sat on the opposite end with his legs crossed in a figure four. She kicked off her hiking boots and stretched out her legs across the sofa cushions. Her pose created a barrier between them, but not a very effective one. When he caught hold of her bare foot and lightly massaged the sole, she felt the tingling effect throughout her body. *Pull your foot back.* But, oh my God, his touch felt good.

She forced herself to focus. What were they talking about? Oh yeah, getting to know him. "Let's start with your unusual name," she said. "Aloysius Periwinkle Carter IV. Why?"

"The name is sick, and not in a good way. Could be that my family is a gang of sadists."

"Who was the first Aloysius and where did he come from?"

"According to our romanticized family history, he was Scotch-Irish and immigrated to Virginia with others from his clan. He was a poet—a worthless job that went well with the fancy Periwinkle part of his name."

"The periwinkle is a flowering vine, common to Europe and North America. Sometimes called the myrtle." She knew her botany. "Mildly poisonous with some medicinal properties."

"A good description of my family," he said.

"One of the common varieties has beautiful blue flowers."

He opened his eyes wide, showing off the color of the iris, which could, in fact, be called periwinkle blue. "Another family trait that's been passed down."

With his index finger, he drew a line down her foot from her middle toe to her heel and back again. A tremor climbed her leg to her hip, stimulating the sciatic nerve, which was the longest and largest in the entire body. She tensed and released, tensed and released and forced her voice to remain calm. "How did the original Aloysius get from Virginia to Colorado?"

"In addition to being called a poet, he was an adventurer. As a young man, he packed up his kilt and headed west during the Pike's Peak gold rush, hoping to make his fortune."

A familiar story. Many of the early pioneers hoped to strike it rich—the same type of naive people who believed in Brighton's Bullion—and many were disappointed. "What did he end up doing instead?"

"A. P. Carter didn't fail. He found a mother lode near Cripple Creek and partnered up with an engineer who knew how to build a functional mine. That partner was his first bit of luck. The second was his wife, an accountant. She wisely invested their profits and made them all rich. Carter started a newspaper in Colorado Springs and opened a pub."

His gentle narrative washed over her and lulled her into a pleasant mood while his clever fingers teased her foot and kept her trembling with awareness. "They had four children, and the oldest male was named for his father. The tradition passed down to my dad. And to me."

"I hope you don't plan to carry Aloysius forward with your firstborn." She'd never saddle her son with such a jawbreaker name. *Her son?* As if she had any reason to think of having children with Carter? *What's wrong with me?*

"Are you all right, Daisy?"

She exhaled a long sigh, almost a groan. "So you inherited the name and the eye color. What else was passed down?"

"A whole lot of money. Investment in Colorado property, especially near Aspen before the ski lodge and real estate boom, paid off nicely. The Carter clan has always done well for themselves financially." His voice took on a ragged, rough edge. "They weren't so lucky when it came to genetics."

Alarmed, she focused on his profile. "An illness?"

"You could say that." He stared down at the arch of her right foot. "Alcoholism. We have a lot of drunks in the family, including my younger brother, Theodore, and our dad."

His charming story about the wandering Scotsman who found gold in them thar hills turned dark and foreboding. She had an idea about the origin of his bitter statement when they realized Gerald Wolff mistreated his son. Carter commented about how abuse didn't excuse bad behavior.

"And you?" She might as well come right out and ask. "Are you an alcoholic?"

"I dodged that bullet." He held up his china teacup and toasted her. "Some might say I controlled my impulses by concentrating on professions that strictly define right and wrong. Studied law in college but changed my mind and went to the Denver Police Academy instead. Dad hated my decision. He never held a steady job and bounced from one supposedly great opportunity to another. Some weren't exactly legal. Worse, he dragged Theo along with him."

"Did they stay in Colorado?"

"Moved to Idaho after my mother divorced the old man." His well-shaped lips curved in a sardonic grin. "I guess I managed to turn out okay. After some serious rehab, Theo also got his act together. He's running the ranch in Idaho, raising cattle. One day at a time."

"I'm sorry," she said, "for all you had to go through."

"While we're on the topic of unhappy twists of fate, I should mention my marriage that lasted less than two years. She hated being married to a cop, and I can't say that I blamed her. After we split, I focused on becoming a ranger. Best job I ever had."

"And you never want to change?" She heard her voice rise on the last word, turning her statement into a question. A hopeful question. Was there a chance for them?

"I didn't think so. Not until recently."

Her spirits lifted. "Recently?"

After one last squeeze of her toes, he placed her feet onto the sofa, stood and went to the whiteboard where they had been trying—futilely—to bring order to their findings. "There's another way we can look at this data. We have four victims, enough to form a pattern."

She had the distinct impression that he had changed the subject as a way to avoid continuing the conversation about his personal life. Discussing the past wasn't easy, and she was willing to play along. "Okay, what kind of pattern are you talking about?

"You're the scientist. What kind of statistics should we use? Some kind of graph or a ranking?"

"We could try a four-way Venn diagram," she said. "Four circles with one section to represent an intersection with all four."

He flipped the whiteboard to the back side, which was blank. He started their diagram with the most recent victim: Rene Williams. While Carter drew a circle and filled in the pertinent data about her, Daisy padded across the hardwood floor to the board in front of his desk and did circles for the other victims.

Next, they filled in the overlapping details. Three had been found in cemeteries. Two were students. Hannah and Andrea had both been employed full-time and lived in the Glenwood Springs area. Three had died from exsanguination due to a slashed carotid, but Eileen was strangled.

The central overlap that showed similarities for all four had only a few notations: All in their twenties. All the bodies were found outdoors.

"It's not much," he said.

"We don't even know their horoscope signs." Daisy turned to him. "What's yours?"

"Aquarius, the deep-thinking loner. Let me guess yours."

Though she didn't believe in the zodiac, she appreciated all the charts and data that had been collected based on date of birth. "Go ahead, guess."

"Scorpio," he said with a seductive smile. "The sexiest sign."

Bingo! She'd heard that thumbnail sketch before and didn't really believe she was a sexy bombshell. "Scorpios are also creative and good with numerical calculations."

"But mostly sexy," he said as he looked at the whiteboard. "We need to go deeper in our analysis. Just like you did with me."

"You and I will never understand how the mind of a serial killer works..." *Thank God for that.*

"...but we can break down the logical pieces and maybe put the puzzle together."

"You lost me."

Daisy was a teacher. She could explain. "Take Hannah, for example. She met up with the killer because he conned her into taking him to Doc Holliday's grave at night. What sort of woman agrees to such a risk?" She answered her own question. "I hate to admit that it could be someone like me, someone who agrees to go for a ride with Jackknife Jones. I guess I'm gullible, too."

Realization dawned in his periwinkle-blue eyes. "And Rene Williams hung out with Slade at Teacup Lake because she thought she was helping him solve a girlfriend problem."

"Again, gullible." She bobbed her head. "We don't know what the killer might have said to Andrea in the grocery store parking lot, because there were no witnesses."

"I read about a scam used by Ted Bundy," Carter said. "He'd approach a woman in a mall or a parking lot and tell her that he needed a woman's help, doing something like taking a child to the bathroom or choosing a color of paint. He played on their sympathies."

"That leaves Eileen, and we don't know enough about her. Tomorrow, when I sit in on the autopsy with Dr. Julia, she might be able to tell me about Eileen Findlay."

"And I can call the tribal police," he said. "We have a good working relationship."

Finally, they seemed to be making progress. The killer stalked his victims, found women who appealed to him and used their gullible/sympathetic nature to lure them into his grasp. She shuddered. These supposed facts—based on inductive reasoning—didn't calm her fears the way she'd hoped they would. She still saw the killer as a monster. A predator. A sociopath.

From the kitchen, she heard her ringtone and dashed to answer. Fortunately, her cell phone was perched at the top of her duffel. She answered, "Hello?"

"Hi, Daisy. I hope it's not too late."

The voice was familiar, but she couldn't quite place it. "Who's this?"

"It's me. Brandi Thoreau." *Slade's girlfriend?* "There's something I need to talk to you about."

WHILE CARTER CLEANED up the tea tray and cups, he eavesdropped on Daisy's phone conversation and heard the tone of her voice shift from frightened to concerned. Her idea about determining similar personality traits of the victims had given him another way to look at their serial killer. He went after empathetic women who could be lured into dangerous situations. Such a person fit Dr. Julia's lessons about victimology. What else did they have in common? All young, all found outdoors, three out of the four were in cemeteries...what else?

More importantly, how did Daisy fit into this picture?

Tonight, on the drive from Pueblo, another vehicle had followed them. *A stalker?* Stalking might be part of the killer's standard procedure. Both Andrea Lindstrom and Hannah Guerrero had mentioned that they felt like someone had been watching them. Most definitely, Daisy had been stalked by Eric Wolff, who admitted using electronic devices to keep track of her whereabouts. Why? And why was a stalker after Daisy? What had she done? Why was she like the others?

He heard her on the phone making plans to meet Brandi for lunch tomorrow outside the building where the autopsy would be done. And then she ended the call.

Still hungry, he took a package of chocolate chip cookies from the upper shelf beside the sink and made a short stack of four. "What's up with Slade's girlfriend?"

"She thinks he's cheating on her because he takes off for hours at a time and doesn't tell her where he's going. Sounds suspicious, right? And Brandi wants me to investigate."

Based on his first impression of Brandi, Carter figured she had the cleverness to run a vlog and be an influencer but not a whole lot of intelligence. "Does she know you're a high school science teacher and not a cop?"

"She seems to think that you and I are working on the same case, and I'm some kind of law enforcement, probably FBI. A compliment, really."

"And you agreed to meet her."

"After the autopsy at one o'clock." She stood and slung her paisley duffel over her shoulder. "We need to return to Pueblo early. It's best if we get some sleep."

Though he didn't want the night to end with Daisy tucked into the queen bed in the guest room, which was far away from the extra-long king that took up half the floor space in the primary bedroom, he didn't know how to switch the topic. He couldn't come right out and ask if she wanted to have sex. Too creepy. Sweeping her into his arms for a passionate kiss didn't work for him, and he couldn't think of any suave, seductive lines to charm her off her feet. He was a forest ranger, dammit. Not smooth. Not clever. Just a guy.

Following her through the house to the staircase, he watched the subtle sway of her hips and the bouncy swing of her curly ponytail. Her energy and vitality made her a pleasure to be around, and he wanted to let her know how much he appreciated her. *Tell her.* The words stuck in his throat. Talking about a serial killer felt easier. *Safer?*

"The feds are going to serve their warrants on Wolff and Slade first thing tomorrow," he said.

"We ought to have preliminary results by lunchtime."

She paused on the staircase and looked down at him. "That means Brandi could hear something about the evidence before our lunch date. Slade might be cleared of suspicion."

"Or not."

"It's weird, you know. We're investigating her boyfriend for murder, and she couldn't care less. She's worried about him being unfaithful."

"Not so strange." He moved up one stair step nearer to her. "If she actually thought he was a killer, she'd run."

"How could she not know?"

"Dr. Jekyll and Mr. Hyde," he reminded her. Sometimes, a heinous murderer lived in the same body as a gentleman.

Her lips parted as though she had more to add, but she stopped speaking. Her opaque green eyes widened as she gazed at him. They stood so close together that he could smell the minty scent of her shampoo, feel the warmth from her body and see the rise and fall of her breathing. A soft pink blush colored her cheeks. Gently, he touched her arm. When she didn't bolt away from him, he tilted toward her.

Her attitude mirrored his. He could feel her attraction rising and mingling with his own, but instead of relaxing into his embrace, she stiffened. Quickly turning away from him, she dashed up the last few stairs and stood on the landing with her gaze darting from one side to the other, not knowing which way to go. His bedroom was at the front of the house to the left. Diagonal to that was the larger of two guest rooms.

He gestured toward the rear of the house. "That way. The bathroom is over here to your left."

Without a word, she disappeared into the bedroom, turned on the light and closed the door. Tonight, nothing would happen between them. He accepted that condition, but it was hard to accept the disappointment. "Good night, Daisy."

Carter went into his bedroom and quietly closed the door. Without turning on the light, he crossed the Berber carpet to his extra-long bed, sat on the edge and pulled off his boots. After a day like this one, he should have been exhausted. And yet, when he lay back on the chocolate-brown duvet, he knew sleep wouldn't come easily. Details about the investigation marched through his mind, making vague and tenuous connections. And then there was Daisy.

She was attracted to him. He knew it. When she looked at him, he saw a warm invitation in her amazing green eyes. In her ever-logical voice, he heard the promise of intimacy. And on the very few occasions when they touched, the sensual chemistry raced through him like a lit fuse.

She liked him but had decided they shouldn't start something they couldn't finish, and the two of them—both adults with fulfilling careers in different locations—weren't permanent relationship material. Could a city gal love a mountain man? Vice versa?

He heard the gush of water in the shower next to his bedroom and groaned as he imagined her, beautifully naked, stepping into the glass enclosure while steam from the hot water billowed around her. Not usually a drinker, he found himself craving a shot of tequila.

This had to stop. He pushed off the bed and stalked toward the glow of moonlight from the dormer. From the second-floor window of his cabin, which was at the top of a small ridge, he had a clear view of his garage, the mailboxes and the road that led past his cabin. Peering into the forest, he noticed movement. A dark shadow, nearly indistinguishable, crept through the trees.

The stalker had returned.

Chapter Seventeen

Carter stood motionless at the dormer window and stared, watching the dangerous shadow slip through the trees on the opposite side of the road. The mysterious dark form melted into the dark silhouette of a jagged boulder. The stalker didn't have a flashlight and wore a baseball cap to cover his hair. The surrounding trees, rocks and leafy shrubs hid his height and size. Though moonlight illuminated the forest, Carter hadn't caught a single glimpse of his face.

Since he knew every inch of these woods and had hiked from the foot of the canyon to the highest point on the cliffs above his cabin, he had an advantage. But he couldn't leave Daisy alone in the cabin, not even with the doors locked. Carter needed backup.

Staying at the window, he took out his phone and hid the screen so the light wouldn't attract attention. He called his boss, who lived nearby. "Joaquin, I've got a problem."

"What's up?" The big man's voice rumbled. "Where are you?"

"Daisy and I are at my cabin. There's a stalker outside in the forest. I need your help."

"Tell me what you wat me to do."

"Park outside my garage, come to the front door

and let yourself in." He gave Joaquin the code to bypass the alarm and told him to go into the kitchen. "You take care of Daisy. I'll go after the stalker."

They didn't waste time with more talk. Carter ended the call, returned his phone to his pocket and looked toward the bathroom. The shower was off, and he heard Daisy humming. Now came the hard part. He had to tell her that her worst fears had come true—the imaginary monster she feared had materialized.

He tapped on the bathroom door. "Daisy, open up."

"Not a good time, Carter."

"I need to talk to you. Now."

When she peeked around the edge of the door, he saw that she'd wrapped herself in a fluffy blue towel. Her damp hair curled around her face. "What is it?" she asked impatiently.

He couldn't explain, couldn't be expected to make sense while standing here talking to a half-naked woman. "Get dressed. Joaquin is coming over. He's on his way."

"What's wrong?"

"The alarm system will be engaged. Don't touch it." He turned away from the door. "Hurry."

He heard the bathroom door slam as he returned to his post at the dormer window. After peering into the forest for a moment, he once again spotted the shadow, still lurking. Carter needed to be prepared for whatever came next. He put on a pair of lightweight hiking boots and a dark gray jacket from his closet. Then he armed himself with his Beretta automatic and an extra clip in the holster attached to his belt. Still not turning on the bedroom light, he fished around in the top drawer of his dresser until he touched a knit cap, which he pulled over his black hair. In his bedside table, he found a tin of black camouflage paint that he smeared across his cheekbones and around his jaw to eliminate the reflection of moonlight on his face.

He saw Daisy approaching on the landing, wearing nothing but a long T-shirt."

Don't turn on the light," he said.

"Why do you have goop on your face?"

"The stalker is here. I saw him on the other side of the road."

She gasped in surprise. Her eyes flickered with panic. "What should we do?"

"I contacted Joaquin to act as backup, and he's on his way. When he gets here, he'll come directly into the house and go to the kitchen. He'll stay here with you."

"And you? What about you?"

"Right now, I'm going outside to position myself. After Joaquin gets here, I'll go after the stalker."

She swayed and braced herself against the doorjamb. "Don't go."

Gently, he eased her into his arms and held her, hoping to shelter her from the fear that had become reality. "This might be my best chance to nab this guy."

Her freshly washed hair smelled of vanilla and orange blossom. Not a fragrance he'd ever used; she must have purchased shampoo at the store. That light, feminine scent would stay with him forever. "Joaquin will be here. You'll be okay."

She exhaled a shuddering breath, then separated from him, stepping backward onto the well-lit landing. When she lifted her chin, he saw a blush rising from her throat. Her green eyes hardened with determination. "Come back to me, Carter. You have to come back."

He didn't know the magic words to assuage her fear. And so, he talked about strategy. "I'll go downstairs first. Right now, the lights are off in the kitchen. After I go out the back door and reset the alarm, you go to the kitchen, turn on the light and wait for Joaquin."

Before he could take a step toward the staircase, she caught hold of his sleeve. She clasped both of his arms, went up on her tiptoes and kissed him on the mouth with an outpouring of passion that had been building all night—actually, it had been building from the moment they met.

Her soft lips contrasted the pressure of her kiss. Her breasts crushed against his chest, and her hips joined with his. Unintentionally, she was making this moment more difficult. He didn't want to leave her. But he had to try to catch this stalker.

Tearing himself away from her, he rushed down the staircase and through the house. Carter didn't breathe until he'd gone out the kitchen door and re-activated the alarm system. The fresh, cool night air brushed his cheeks but did nothing to douse the fire she'd started in his heart. Their connection felt deeper than any attraction that might develop in a few days. He didn't believe in fate or kismet or any of that other romantic stuff, but he couldn't help a rising belief that they were meant to be together.

Yeah, great...but before the big, dramatic love scene got underway, he needed to catch a serial killer.

He ducked into the forest, taking a narrow path that led uphill, where he'd have a better view. Crouched behind a large, flat-topped boulder, he peered past his cabin to the opposite side of the road. The shadowy figure had barely moved. *Should have brought my rifle.* Though Carter didn't have a clear shot, he had skills as a marksman. He could make this shot.

His thinking recalibrated. *I'm not a sniper. Not a murderer.* His job was to apprehend this man and bring him to justice. To keep him from harming more women.

He heard Joaquin's Range Rover approaching and saw him pull into the driveway. Carter kept his gaze trained on the seemingly motionless shadow across the road. The stalker dodged the Rover's headlights, then stood to watch when his boss parked in front of the closed garage door. Joaquin climbed out and strode up the inclined pathway to the door.

Though Carter couldn't see the front porch from where he hunkered down on the hillside, he heard the door close and assumed Joaquin had gone inside. How would the stalker react? Settle back and wait? Try to sneak close and peek through windows? Or would he run?

If he ran, which way would he go? Probably, he'd left his vehicle down the hill on his way to the cabin. There were several turnoffs and wide shoulders where he could have parked. Carter counted on the stalker going left, which was why he'd taken a position on the left side of his cabin. He was ready.

The muscles in his thighs tensed as he crept from behind the boulder. He wanted to get as close as possible before he made a charge. One silent step after another, he went downhill.

For no apparent reason, the stalker jolted into action…but he didn't go left. Instead, he jogged through the trees, heading up the road to higher ground.

Carter had to move fast. Still trying to be quiet, he broke into a run, dodging through trees and over rocks. About a hundred yards from his cabin, the road swerved. When the stalker reached that point, he'd be out of direct sight. In the moonlight, he saw the shadowy figure race around the curve.

Carter hit the road and turned up the speed. After struggling to find his footing on the forested hillside, the two-lane graded gravel road was a relief. Carter broke into a sprint. In seconds, he rounded the curve. To his right, a driveway led to his neighbor's cabin. Didn't look like anybody was home. He kept running uphill, careening around another twist in the road.

In the stillness of the night, he heard a car engine start up. *He's getting away.* Several yards ahead, he saw the unlit taillights of a car, driving fast and swerving. At the next zigzag in the road, the lights came on. The vehicle swiveled into the turn and disappeared.

Breathing heavily, Carter stopped in the center of the road. He stared at the turn where the taillights had been. Frustration poured over him. He hadn't seen the license place. Didn't know what kind of vehicle he was chasing. Those red lights hadn't belonged to a truck or a van—just a regular sedan like thousands of others on the road. His sighting of the stalker hadn't moved the investigation forward one bit.

He had to wonder if he'd actually seen anything. Was he so desperate to find answers that he'd invented a stalker the same way Daisy imagined monsters? He tilted his head up toward the thousands of diamond-bright stars scattered across the dark sky. They seemed to be laughing at him. In his black cap and camo makeup, did he look as ridiculous as he felt?

Jogging down the road, he went to the place he thought he'd seen the watcher. Behind a waist-high boulder, the grasses were trampled and branches on shrubs had been snapped. He took out the compact Maglite attached to his key chain and shone the beam around the area. The light showed him a flash of color. A long scarf in yellow and orange draped over a shrub.

No doubt about it. The stalker had gotten the last laugh.

AS SOON AS Daisy heard Carter at the front door, she hopped off the kitchen stool and darted toward the sound. Joaquin followed, and she suspected he stayed close to protect her in case the person at the door wasn't Carter after all. The big man who ran the Salida headquarters for the National Park Service was about as subtle as a grizzly bear when it came to bodyguard work, but she appreciated his honest concern. Shortly after they'd met, he busied himself in the kitchen brewing herbal tea and talking about organics and the garden outside his cabin, where he cultivated indigenous Colorado plants, like wild onion, asparagus and skunk cabbage. He believed in living off the land. As a biology teacher, she totally agreed.

When Carter stepped through the door, she wrapped herself around him. If he'd been injured while trying to protect her, she would never have forgiven herself. She loosened her grip long enough for him to disarm and reset the alarm.

"In case you're wondering," Joaquin said, "you were never in real danger. If the intruder had tried to break in, Carter's alarms and my physical presence would have protected you. If all that failed, Carter would step in. He doesn't look tough, but our guy is kind of a badass."

"Takes one to know one," Carter murmured.

"I'm guessing the stalker got away," Joaquin said. "Any new evidence?"

Instead of answering Joaquin, Carter concentrated on Daisy, as though he was assessing her state of mind. "Maybe it's best if—"

"You can talk in front of me." Daisy wanted to know if her panic had any basis in reality. "How about this? You tell us what you found, then go wash the goop off your face."

"Fair enough." He glanced between her and Joaquin. "He took off before I could catch him, but I caught a glimpse of his taillights. It wasn't Slade's camper truck or the Wolff painting van. He was driving a regular compact sedan."

"A second car," Joaquin said.

"He was too far away for me to recognize the make or see a license plate." Carter shrugged. "I came back to the place where I'd seen him hiding. The grasses were trampled, branches broken, and I found this."

From the inner pocket of his jacket, he pulled out a plastic evidence bag. Inside was a silky scarf with streaks of orange, peach and yellow like a mountain sunrise.

Daisy turned her head and looked away. "I hate that he left this. Like a taunt."

"That's the reaction he wants," Joaquin said. "Part of the serial killer profile is narcissism. He's asserting his superiority by literally waving a flag in your face, daring you to catch him."

"Why?" She clenched her fists. "Why us?"

"My guess? He sees Carter as an adversary. I'm not sure why he's after you, but he is. It's almost like he's obsessed."

"Joaquin's good with profiles," Carter said. "This old hippie has spent much of his life studying people. He was a therapist before he joined the park service."

She'd already guessed the hippie part from the faded Ramones T-shirt under his uniform. Looking to him for an answer, she asked, "More specifically, why me? Why is this person coming after me?"

"Let's talk about it," he said, sounding like a therapist as he took her arm and guided her toward the kitchen. "Carter, you go wash your face. The camo makeup makes me think you should be in hand-to-hand combat with a gang of video game mercenaries."

Back in the kitchen, Joaquin freshened her tea

and sat beside her at the black granite–topped island. He stirred a teaspoon of raw sugar crystals into his tea. "Before Carter comes back, I want to tell you about a phone call I got earlier tonight."

Daisy groaned. "Let me guess. My aunt Violet."

"Violet Rhodes of Leadville," he confirmed. "She's concerned about your safety and wanted a character reference on Carter."

"I'm sorry she bothered you."

"Not a bit." He smiled. "We talked awhile, shared a couple of gardening tips, and she grilled me about the weapons I carry."

"A long time ago, she had a peeper and bought a handgun for self-defense." She exhaled a sigh. "That was how her arsenal got started."

He stroked his salt-and-pepper beard. "After our conversation, I looked her up on the computer. She has a beautiful house and a very nice…garden."

Joaquin personified the sort of man Aunt Vi liked. Educated and healthy with a good job, plus he wore a uniform. Daisy ought to warn him before he became Vi's husband number five.

Carter strolled into the kitchen, wiping the last vestiges of camo makeup off his face with a towel. "What are you two talking about?"

"Daisy's aunt," Joaquin said. "She's coming to Salida tomorrow to look into the serial killer situation, and I promised to show her around in Pueblo."

Though Daisy would be delighted to have Joaquin involved in the FBI investigation, she really didn't like the idea of Aunt Vi being close. "Do you think it's dangerous for her to come?"

"I'll just have to protect her," Joaquin said. He turned to Carter. "Have you met the lady?"

"I have, indeed."

"Let me ask you, is Violet Rhodes a woman who likes a man who chops his own wood?"

"Wait and see."

Chapter Eighteen

The next morning, Daisy and Carter hit the road by seven o'clock. He'd brewed fresh coffee and filled two silver travel mugs. The excellent coffee and an energy bar she'd already gobbled up provided all the breakfast she wanted. After the excitement last night, Daisy hadn't expected to get a good night's sleep, but as soon as her head nestled into the pillow in the guest room, she sank into a deep slumber and didn't waken until Carter roused her this morning.

Holding her mug with both hands, she took a sip and quietly relived the moment when her eyelids had fluttered open and she'd seen him sitting on the edge of her bed—showered, sexy and shirtless. The sunrise had cut through a split in the blue plaid curtains to highlight his lips and his high cheekbones. The blue in his eyes was as deep and pure as...periwinkle flowers.

Her waking thought had been that she was dreaming, but then he'd kissed her forehead with a light pressure that, nonetheless, sent a buzz through her nerve endings. She'd pulled him down on top of her for a deeper kiss. Her hands had stroked his warm, well-muscled chest. More, she'd wanted more. But common sense had reared its ugly head, and she'd rolled away from him.

She raised her mug to her lips, took another sip and turned her head to study his profile as he drove. "What's going to happen after the investigation is wrapped up?"

"We take things one day at a time," he said. "The drive from Leadville to Salida is a couple of hours, not far enough to count whatever we have going on here as a long-distance relationship. We can still see each other."

"In a month, I'll be back at my regular job in Denver. My time at Aunt Vi's is temporary." She recalled their conversation last night. "Speaking of my aunt, what did Joaquin mean when he asked about chopping wood?"

"Recently, he told me that his ex-wife liked to watch when he cut logs for their fireplace." Carter grinned and wiggled his eyebrows. "Watching him get all sweaty made her horny."

"Oh, that's not good. He's thinking about Aunt Vi and sex before he even meets her. Once he gets the full flirting treatment, the poor guy doesn't stand a chance."

"He's not helpless, you know."

"But my aunt is really good at teasing and making men fall for her, even Jackknife Jones. Seduction is kind of her superpower."

His ringtone sounded, and he answered the cell phone attached to the dashboard. "Good morning, Agent Wiley. I have you on speaker. Daisy is in the car with me."

"FYI, we're in the process of serving a warrant at Slade Franklin's house. Forensic techs are crawling all over the place, and our boy Slade isn't happy."

"Didn't think he would be."

"We've already turned up evidence in his camper truck. A pair of pink cotton underpants and several long brown hairs."

Daisy's pulse beat faster as she remembered the first time she saw Rene Williams at the cemetery with her long brown hair fanned out around her head. "It's Rene."

"About the panties," Carter said. "Slade has a girlfriend."

"We've met, and she's almost as mad as her boyfriend. Not about him being a suspect, but she flew into a rage when she heard about the panties in his camper truck. She said they weren't hers. Apparently, she doesn't wear cotton. Only silk."

"Did she spend the night with Slade last night?"

"She was working as an internet influencer—whatever that is—until midnight at the opening of a new tavern, then she came to this house and stayed the rest of the night."

Daisy nodded. The timing made sense. If Slade had been stalking the cabin last night, he might have rushed home to meet Brandi, who gave him an alibi. "Anything else?" she asked. "I don't suppose you found blood."

"No such luck," Wiley said, "but we're impounding the vehicle for a closer inspection. Slade has serious objections. He uses his truck for work, and he's scheduled to be at a church renovation all week."

"Does he have another vehicle?" Carter asked.

"A 2012 Toyota Corolla. Not a lot of trunk space, but he can transport most of his tools."

She exchanged a glance with Carter. Slade might have been driving the four-door Toyota last night. The more they learned about him, the more suspicious he looked.

"Thanks for calling," Carter said to Wiley. "After I drop Daisy off at the autopsy suite with Dr. Julia, I'll be in touch."

When he disconnected the call, they were driving past the NPS headquarters in Salida. She saw only one SUV with the NPS logo in the small asphalt lot. Joaquin's car? Last night, he'd told her that Aunt Vi expected to be in Salida early this morning. She hadn't seen fit to contact Daisy with an update. *Typical!* Her aunt had scented adventure in the air and wanted to be a part of it.

"It's too bad Slade has an explanation for those hairs and panties," Carter said. "The first time we talked to him, he told us that he and Rene went skinny-dipping in Teacup Lake. She changed clothes in his camper truck. It's possible she dropped a pair of panties."

Daisy would check the inventory of Rene's clothing from the autopsy to discover if she was wearing underwear when she was killed. Not that it made much difference. She might have left the panties a day or two before her murder.

"When we found Rene's body," she said, "she was barefoot, and her feet were clean, which meant she hadn't been walking through the forest. Maybe she'd just come from skinny-dipping with Slade. He might have slashed her throat while they were in the water, let her bleed out and carried her to shore, where he dressed her."

Images from that scenario flashed through her mind like a horror movie. She hated the way her imagination conjured up these scary pictures.

"I think you're onto something," Carter said. "Slade is a muscular guy. He wouldn't have any trouble carrying a petite woman like Rene. Did the autopsy show she'd been in the water?"

"She wasn't drowned." Daisy squeezed her eyes shut, trying to banish the mental image of tall, rangy Slade carrying the lifeless body of Rene through the trees. "He'd have to be naked, of course. So he wouldn't get blood on his clothes."

"Are you visualizing the scene?"

"I am." Her throat tightened. "It's horrifying."

"You have a talent, Daisy. I know you consider your imagination to be a curse, but it's also a gift. With the way you think, you could be a terrific detective."

But she didn't want to solve crimes. Involvement in the serial murders had showed her a peek behind the curtain separating civil behavior from nightmare insanity, and she had no desire to go deeper. She lifted the coffee mug to her lips and took another swallow. "I'll leave the detecting to others, thank you very much."

"Don't you want to catch the bad guys and see justice done?"

"Of course I do. But not by scaring myself half to death." She changed the topic. "Where should I take Brandi for lunch? You're a foodie. Give me some suggestions."

"I'm guessing the big-deal influencer will know where she wants to go. When you know where you're headed, text me. I'll join you."

"I hope she's not blaming us for the FBI raid this morning."

Daisy expected Brandi to be angry about the warrants and the search. It might be best to check with her before lunch. Until then, she intended to take a deep dive into practical anatomy, watching Dr. Julia perform the autopsy on Andrea Lindstrom.

AFTER CARTER PARKED and escorted Daisy to the door of the building where the autopsy would be performed, he texted SAC Wiley. The forensic team was in the process of serving Gerald Wolff with a warrant to search his vehicles and his home. Wiley invited Carter to join them.

When he parked in front of the Wolffs' house, he

needed no introduction to recognize Gerald Wolff, who sprawled on the front porch of a two-story grayish house that was—ironically—in desperate need of a paint job. One of the front windows had been broken and patched with duct tape and cardboard. An aura of disrepair and neglect hung over the property.

In his worn cotton bathrobe, sleeveless T-shirt and striped boxer shorts, Gerald Wolff matched the unkempt house. His short white hair stuck out in spikes. The grungy plaid robe barely covered his belly. An oxygen tank sat beside him, and a cannula hooked into his bulbous nose. Daisy had mentioned the reddened complexion common to heavy drinkers, and Carter agreed with her diagnosis.

Gerald squinted at him and demanded, "Who the hell are you?"

He pointed to the bison badge fastened to his belt. "National Park Service."

Realization dawned in Gerald's small, piggy eyes. "You're the park ranger who hangs out with Daisy. She attacked me, you know."

Carter had no problem seeing this angry, hostile old man as a murderer, but he couldn't picture Gerald lifting and carrying the victims or tying silk scarves around their throats. Sad to say, he didn't have the macabre style of this serial killer.

SAC Wiley opened the front screen door and motioned for Carter to come inside. "There's something you've got to see."

When Carter walked around the old man, he caught a whiff of the whiskey in his coffee. Inside the house, he wasn't surprised to see stacks of magazines and unopened mail. Used plates and mugs were scattered across coffee tables and on chairs. In spite of a central air-conditioning system and ceiling fans, the stench of rotting garbage mingled with the smell of turpentine from jars holding used paintbrushes.

He followed Wiley up the staircase, where the clutter persisted in a large bedroom. The covers and sheets were tangled in a wad at the foot of the bed. The bedside table held no fewer than four empty bottles of generic-brand whiskey. No doubt, Gerald's room. Across the landing, Eric's room seemed to have been transported from a different home. Tidy, dusted and vacuumed, the shelves held a neat array of books and photos, including several of Eric as a small, towheaded boy standing with a smiling woman who much have been his mom. Other photos showed his golden retriever. A flat-screen television sat beside a desktop computer.

"An amazing contrast," Carter said. "Looks like Eric went out of his way to be as different from his father as possible."

"Not entirely." Back on the upstairs landing, he pointed Carter toward a closed door. "See for yourself."

In a small room, not much bigger than a walk-in closet, Eric had made an office with file cabinets and a narrow table that stretched all the way across one wall—a wall entirely covered with corkboard. Opposite, he'd hung a detailed map of southwestern Colorado with several locations marked by colored pushpins. Another table held a laptop and printer to create photographs from his phone. Eric had been busy. Dozens of photos of landscapes—lush hillsides, oddly shaped boulders and trees—decorated the corkboard.

After a brief study, Carter recognized the forest outside Butcher's Gulch. He saw the fence surrounding Doc Holliday's grave marker. These were photos of cemeteries.

Scattered among the graveyards, photos of people popped up at random. A picture of Violet Rhodes showed her at an outdoor shooting range wearing ear protection and aiming a tiny Glock 19. Several snapshots of an older woman who resembled the person Carter assumed was Eric's mother lined the right edge of the wall. There was one of Jackknife Jones, looking like a bum. Three photos of Daisy centered on the wall in a triangle. In one, she had a dreamy look in her green eyes as she leaned against the porch banister outside her aunt Vi's house. Another caught her in action, running toward the entrance of the FBI building. The third picture had been taken at Teacup Lake, when Daisy had melted into Carter's embrace and they kissed.

Chapter Nineteen

Daisy observed Dr. Julia's skillful technique as she opened the skull of Andrea Lindstrom while preserving the damage done to her face and neck by animal predators. Previously, Dr. Julia had confirmed Daisy and Carter's hypothesis about Andrea being placed in the shallow grave at Butcher's Gulch and wrapped in a drop cloth, which the coyotes and other animals tore open. The really important discovery from this autopsy had been the presence of immature ten-lined June beetles in Andrea's ears and her other wounds. This species wasn't found in the higher elevation of Glenwood Springs and probably not at Butcher's Gulch. The ten-lined beetle was common in high desert areas like Pueblo.

Daisy couldn't wait to tell Carter. The beetle gave them tangible evidence that Andrea had been taken from Glenwood and brought to this area, where she might have been held for the three days between when she disappeared and when her body turned up at Butcher's Gulch. The killer might have a lair in this area. *A lair?* She shuddered at the thought and hoped the FBI searches at the Wolff house and Slade's might show where Andrea—and possibly others—had been held.

Other autopsy findings: faint ligature marks on

her ankles and wrists, which indicated the use of restraints, but not in a painful way. She hadn't been handcuffed or duct-taped. There were no signs of torture. They found puncture wounds from a hypodermic needle.

The tox screen showed Andrea had been drugged as well as zapped with a stun gun. During that three-day period, sedatives could have been used to keep her quiet and under control but not unconscious.

The time for Daisy's noon appointment with Brandi was rapidly approaching. Though she hated to leave the autopsy suite, where she felt comfortable, Daisy waved goodbye to Dr. Julia and pointed to the time on a wall clock over the door.

Julia nodded. Through her plastic face shield, the doctor smiled. In a talk with Daisy, she'd shared contact information and encouraged her to visit while she was in the mountains. In addition to her responsibilities with autopsies, Julia ran a clinic on the Ute reservation and experimented with the medicinal properties of native plants.

"*Towaoc.*" Daisy whispered the Ute word for "thank you," truly grateful for the opportunity to spend time with this wise, generous woman.

On her way out, Daisy shed her personal protective equipment: mask, gloves, hair covering and suit. She strode through the pleasant waiting room into the hallway and out the door to the parking lot. Carter must have warned her a million times to avoid going anywhere by herself, but just in case, she held her key chain with her trusty pepper spray.

Brandi had arrived earlier and posed beside her cheery yellow Ford SUV that made a pretty contrast with her red, white and blue–striped T-shirt and red mini. Her long mahogany hair was parted in the middle and pulled up into two cute ponytails. She waved to Daisy, pursed her mouth in duck lips and snapped a selfie. Daisy groaned inwardly. *This is going to be a long lunch.*

"Hope you don't mind if I take photos for my vlog," Brandi said. "Is it okay for me to tell people you work for the FBI?"

"I'm a high school science teacher in Denver." Not comfortable with having her face splashed across the internet, she shook her head. "Don't mention the FBI."

"Yeah, right, you're a schoolteacher. Well, that's a snooze."

"Think about it, Brandi. You don't want me to tell all your followers that the FBI served a warrant on Slade, do you?"

"Guess not." She rolled her big brown eyes, clearly bored and frustrated. "What else can I say about you that's interesting? Something cool."

"Brighton's Bullion," Daisy said.

Brandi adored the story about Daisy's ancestor—the outlaw Sherwood Brighton—who left behind a treasure in gold bullion that had never been found. While they drove to Herbivore's, a trendy restaurant on the downtown Pueblo Riverwalk that offered a full vegetarian menu plus twenty-six different flavors of fruit drinks.

"I have a special parking permit," Brandi said as she zipped into a parking slot. "All this week, I'm visiting different locations on Riverwalk, promoting them and vlogging about their specialties."

"Is that where you were last night?"

"Yeah. I asked Slade to come with, but he said no. His loss."

Inside the restaurant, greenery abounded, and the air was redolent with the fragrance of mint, lavender and basil. Daisy ordered a mint iced tea, nonalcoholic.

"It's better with schnapps," Brandi said.

But Daisy didn't want a repeat of yesterday's mild intoxication. She needed to have her wits about her. Following a suggestion from the waitress, she ordered vegetarian lasagna with béchamel sauce. Brandi opted for a beet and broccoli salad with hard cider to drink.

After organizing a simple recording setup with a small camera and lavalier mics for both of them, Brandi asked Daisy to repeat her order into the camera. She did the same, then she clearly described Daisy's claim to the family treasure of gold bullion worth millions of dollars. "Tell me, Daisy Brighton, how big are all those gold bars?"

"It's about enough to fill a steamer trunk."

"Or a coffin." Brandi mugged for the camera. "Is that why you hang around at cemeteries?"

Daisy evaded the potentially dangerous part of that topic by launching into a fact-based discussion about cemeteries in the Old West and boot hill graveyards. Though Brandi kept smiling, Daisy could see the other woman's eyes glaze over. *Another snoozefest.*

When their food came, Brandi took pictures on her phone and engaged the waitress in a conversation about preparation. Finally, she turned off the recording equipment. "Nobody wants to watch us eating," she said. "Or talking with our mouths full."

After tasting the vegetarian lasagna and loving the creamy flavor, Daisy pursued her own line of questions. "You and Slade seem so different. Is he often gone on jobs?"

"He's kind of a loner. On the plus side, he's tall, has a great body and photographs well." She snatched up her phone and flipped to a handsome photo of Slade with his shirt off. On his upper left bicep, he had a heart tattoo that said, "Mama."

"See?"

"You've been dating for a couple of years, right?"

She nodded. "Since before Mama died. But we've broken up a couple of times."

"Were you taking a break from each other when he met Rene Williams?"

"Can you believe that little witch?" Brandi took a swallow of her cider. "Leaving her cheap pink panties in my honey-boo's camper? She didn't waste any time moving in on him."

Apparently, Brandi had never heard the old adage about not speaking ill of the dead. "Are you aware that she was tragically murdered?"

"Yeah, yeah." She rolled her eyes. "Boo-hoo."

Daisy moved to a wider focus. "Have you uncovered other evidence that he's been unfaithful?"

"I found a necklace. Actually, there were two of them, as if he bought one for me and one for some other girl. When I showed the jewelry to him, he said they were both for me. He was trying to decide which he liked best." She rolled her eyes. "But they were identical."

Daisy recalled the heart pendant worn by Eileen Findlay, the Ute woman whose body had been found not far from where they were eating. "What did the necklace look like?"

"A little heart. Cute but kind of chintzy. I wear it when I'm trying to relate to the people who follow my vlogs and podcasts."

Daisy asked, "Did he ever give you a scarf?"

"He tried. Mama was big on scarves, but I don't like them. I'm real careful putting together my outfits and don't want a drapey piece of material covering me up."

She remembered Brandi talking about how Slade had tried to get her to dress like his mother. "His mother kind of ran his life."

"Wasn't a bad deal. She left him a lot of money.

You know, he's weird about being rich. Prefers to pay cash for everything." Brandi paused and looked around the restaurant as though scanning for other influencers who might steal her thunder. "This is why I wanted to talk to you."

"Okay."

"I think Mama left her sonny boy another property outside town."

Daisy felt a spike of adrenaline. "Like his own secret lair?"

"Or a love nest," Brandi said. "I think he goes there on his long weekends and fixes the place up. Then he takes his little girlfriends there."

"Do you know where it is?"

Pushing the beets around on her plate, Brandi shook her head, clearly unhappy about the idea of her honey-boo with another woman. "I need you to help me find it."

"Have you asked him about it?"

"He swears there's no special place. Tells me that I'm his one and only, but I've got a sense about this. Can you use your FBI contacts to find the location?"

"I can try." Though it seemed likely the FBI could turn up an address, she didn't know for sure. "Do you have any other clues about the love nest?"

"The old bat who lives next door to Slade, Mrs. Gallagher, used to be tight with Mama. Hates me, of course. But Slade does little repairs around her house, and she thinks he's wonderful. Could you talk to her?"

"I don't see why not," Daisy said.

She spotted Carter at the door of the restaurant, wearing jeans and a lightweight tan blazer to hide the clip-on holster on his belt. She waved him over. Though she'd checked before inviting him to join them, Daisy noticed that Brandi's expression darkened as she watched Carter's progress. She muttered, "I blame your ranger friend for the FBI raid."

With one hundred percent honesty, Daisy said, "Carter wants what's best for everybody." *Which means finding the serial killer.* "I'm sure he'll help find Slade's secret property." *If only to call in the forensic team.*

"Yeah? Well, okay." Brandi rose to shake hands with Carter. "Wish I could stay, Mr. Ranger, but I've got a full day."

"Nice restaurant," he said. "I've never been here before."

"Lunch is on me." She waved the waitress over and paid with a $100 bill. "Get them whatever they want."

"How can I get in touch with you?" he asked.

"Daisy has my number."

"What about Slade's cell phone?"

"He might answer but probably not. He's doing renovations for a little chapel in the forest. And he never gives me names and numbers for his clients." Before flouncing away from Herbivore's, she gave

Daisy a hug and whispered, "If you find anything about you-know-what, call me."

"I will," Daisy promised. And if Slade turned out to be a killer, she'd make sure Brandi had an appointment with a reputable therapist.

When Carter took a seat beside her at the table, she couldn't tear her gaze away from him. If possible, he seemed to get better looking every time she saw him. "Sorry you didn't get to ask Brandi any questions."

"I didn't expect much. What did she tell you?"

"She wanted me to use my FBI contacts—as if I had any—to find the location of her boyfriend's love nest in a property left to him by his mama. Can we do that?"

"We can ask. If there's a record, we can probably dig it up."

"Hungry?"

Quietly, he said, "I grabbed a burger before I came here. I'm surprised all these noncarnivores can't smell the beef on me."

She took her last bite of the truly delicious lasagna. "Want to get out of here?"

"This is not a good place to discuss serial killers. Too healthy."

They stepped outside into a spectacular, clear, blue-sky day. Not yet as hot as July and August but warm. She was glad to take off her long-sleeved dark blue sweater. As they strolled along the paved path following the winding course of the Arkansas River, a light breeze slid across the water and ruffled the manicured foliage that lined the walk. Bronze statues of bison, antelope and an old-time cowboy on horseback hid among colorful displays of daisies, lavender and sage.

For a carefree moment, she reveled in the scent of fresh-mowed grass and the laughter of kids who chased each other through the park. An involuntary smile lifted the corners of her mouth. On a day like this, with Carter at her side, Daisy felt upbeat and positive. But happiness didn't last forever. The monsters in her imagination hadn't vanished—they were merely hiding.

She turned to him. "You need to know about the ten-lined June beetle."

"Something you found in the autopsy?"

She nodded and explained how the immature beetles were only found in high desert terrain in late spring or early summer, which meant Andrea had been brought to someplace like Pueblo. "Maybe to his lair. She must have been killed here and dead for several hours, which is how the beetles got into her wounds."

"Then he wrapped her in a drop cloth and took her to Butcher's Gulch."

A growing awareness reminded her that another victim had been found on the Riverwalk. Daisy didn't want to know the location—didn't want those dark thoughts to take seed and grow.

"I guess we've pretty much decided that Slade is the killer."

Taking her hand, he pulled her off the walkway to a bench, where they sat, watching the kids playing and the tourists and paddle boats shaped like giant rubber duckies. He cleared his throat. "I have to tell you what the FBI found at the Wolff house."

She braced herself, knowing from his serious expression that this wasn't good news. She lifted the brown cowboy hat from his head so she could see the truth in his periwinkle-blue eyes. "What is it?"

He told her about the office Eric had designed for himself on the second floor of the house—a private space with a corkboard wall where he posted photographs, mostly of outdoor scenery. "Cemeteries. Including the boot hill at Butcher's Gulch and Doc Holliday's grave."

"Murder sites." In spite of the warm sun beating down on her back, her blood ran cold. She laced her fingers with his and held on tight. "What else?"

"There were pictures of a woman I think is his mother, who divorced Gerald. Also, photos of Aunt Vi, Jackknife Jones and you. Three photos of you, including one of us kissing."

All the clues pointing toward Slade crumbled to dust. Here was tangible proof that Eric Wolff was, at the very least, a creepy stalker. At worst… a serial killer.

She inhaled a deep breath, hoping to pump fresh air into her lungs. "Anything else?"

"I talked to Joaquin earlier. Before I left the house, he showed up with your aunt."

Compared with being the star photo on a stalker's corkboard, Aunt Vi's appearance almost counted as good news. "Did they see Eric's office?"

"I managed to keep Vi away from there, even though she demanded full access to everything. I also hid an envelope Eric had addressed to you."

"Isn't that illegal? Tampering with evidence."

"I fully intend to hand it over to Wiley." He reached into the inner pocket of his tan blazer and pulled it out. "I thought you should see it first."

She opened the unsealed envelope and took out a photocopied letter. Like the last one Eric had given to her, this was from Annie Brighton to Morris Wolff. The language of the long-ago lover was graphic and dripping with longing—until she mentioned the bullion.

Daisy read aloud. "'Sherwood thinks he's the boss, but the old fool is utterly wrong. Mark my words. I'll take that gold to the grave with me.'"

She thought of the grave at Butcher's Gulch. They needed to get an exhumation order.

Chapter Twenty

After Carter put in a call to Wiley about tracking down the out-of-town property that Mama Franklin had left to Slade, he and Daisy got back into his SUV and set out to visit Mrs. Gallagher, the neighbor lady who liked Slade but not his girlfriend. These efforts were important but not his primary goal. Everything he did, every motivation, every thought centered on one job: protect Daisy.

Eric the stalker was obsessed with her and a definite threat. Papa Wolff, Gerald, might attack for no other reason than Daisy had zapped him with her pepper spray. As for Slade… Carter didn't know why the mama's boy would be interested in Daisy, but he was dangerous.

When he parked outside Slade's house, he noticed the lack of vehicles. Slade's camper truck—usually in the driveway—had been confiscated by the FBI for further processing. His garage doors were open, showing an empty space where he probably kept his Toyota. And Brandi hadn't returned with her yellow Ford. Nobody was home. *Good.*

As they approached the next-door neighbor's front door, Daisy said, "I think you should do the talking. This lady seems to be partial to men."

Mrs. Gallagher opened the door a few seconds after Carter pressed the doorbell, which made him think she'd been watching and waiting. A tiny woman with a crest of red hair and bright eyes magnified by oversize glasses, she reminded him of a woodpecker. He introduced himself and showed his badge. "Ranger Carter of the NPS. Are you Mrs. Gallagher?"

"A forest ranger, eh?" She squinted up at him. "I saw you next door. And this lady?"

Daisy stuck out her hand. "I'm a high school science teacher."

"Oh, my." Mrs. Gallagher shook hands but wasn't friendly. Her skinny arms wrapped around her middle, and she didn't ask them to come in. "What do you want?"

"We're working with the FBI," Carter said. "And we heard that you were close to the late Mrs. Franklin."

"I'll bet that Brandi girl told you." She sniffed, sticking her nose in the air. "Elizabeth would have despised her. She wanted the best for Slade, and that ain't Miss Brandi, flaunting herself all over the computer. Shameless, that's what she is."

Carter hoped to keep this meeting short, and so he didn't push her to invite them into her house. "Do you know if Elizabeth Franklin owned a property outside town?"

"What if she did?" Mrs. Gallagher stuck out her pointed chin. "There's no law against having four acres of property right near a lake that's full of trout."

"Sounds like you've been there."

"Maybe I have, but not in a long time. The last year before she passed, Elizabeth wasn't up to taking trips. I saw her almost every day, though. Brought her and Slade casseroles and roast beef for sandwiches. Slade loved my snickerdoodle cookies."

Once she got started talking, she didn't have a stop button. He interrupted, "Do you have an address? Can you tell us where the property is located?"

"Sorry, Ranger. I don't see very well, and I didn't drive. It was in a forest. Not the mountains. The name of the lake was Shelby or something like that. Elizabeth's cabin was at the end of a road that was blocked off with a gate and a sign—No Trespassing."

The perfect place for a love nest. Or a villain's lair. "Do you remember anything else?"

"Ask Slade? She left the property to him." She pushed her door open a bit wider. "Say, why don't you come inside and have some cookies and milk?"

He took a step backward, fearful that if they went through that door, they'd never escape. "Thank you, Mrs. Gallagher, you've been very helpful."

"Come back any time." She waved as they walked away.

At the street, Daisy grinned. "I was right. She prefers good-looking men. Did the location of Elizabeth Franklin's cabin sound familiar?"

"Too familiar. There are hundreds of lakes with little cabins and No Trespassing signs." He'd need to cross-reference names of lakes on a map. "Let's check in at the FBI. Maybe they have something more accurate."

The tide of evidence had begun to turn in their direction. Every move they made turned up another piece of the puzzle. When they found Slade's lair/love nest, he hoped they'd uncover evidence that he'd taken the victims to that place. Or not.

"What happened with Aunt Vi and Joaquin?" she asked.

"I'm hoping they went back to Salida, but I doubt it. Your aunt wants to investigate."

"Not surprised," Daisy said. "I'll bet she thinks that if she looked into the case, she could solve it in a snap."

"The opposite. When Vi talked to Wiley and Hicks, she spewed dozens of compliments about the brave FBI. She might even have squeezed Hicks's bicep and giggled."

"Catching more flies with honey than with vinegar," Daisy said. "I told you she was really good at flirting."

Not like her niece. Aunt Vi was beautifully groomed, manicured and polished, while Daisy didn't seem to care about her appearance. Her beauty seemed natural and almost careless. Instead of flirting, Daisy blurted. She managed to get her way but lacked subtlety and skill in manipulating others. Instead, she came right out and said what she thought. Though he liked her straightforward attitude, her rational explanation of why they shouldn't start any kind of physical relationship didn't make him happy. A little flirting might have softened the blow.

Glancing across the console, he noticed the glimmer of sunlight in her blond hair, and he wanted to comb his fingers through the strands that fell from her ponytail and curled around her neck. He appreciated her posture and her sharp attention to all that was going on around her.

"Look over there." She pointed through the passenger-side window. "I know that truck."

"Jackknife Jones." What the hell was the old codger doing in Pueblo? More importantly, why had Carter dismissed him as a suspect? "He doesn't seem to be following us."

She winced. "He could be after Aunt Vi."

Though Carter could have turned on his flashers and forced the beat-up truck to pull over, he'd rather see where Jackknife was headed. "I'm going to follow him."

Apparently, the old man wasn't familiar with traffic patterns in Pueblo, and Carter knew from prior conversations that the aged truck didn't have GPS. They trailed him in a meaningless meander through the streets until he hit the one-way street with the FBI headquarters building. Jackknife zeroed in on his destination. Joaquin's NPS vehicle was parked in front.

"You're right," Carter said. "He's not after you. It's Aunt Vi."

"How would he know where she is?"

"Let's find out."

When Carter turned on his flashers, Jackknife pulled over to the curb in a No Parking area in front. After he parked and told Daisy to stay in the SUV, Carter got out of his car and drew his weapon, following standard procedure. "Show me your hands. Out the window."

Jackknife did as he was ordered. As soon as he saw Carter, he snarled. "You! Again?"

"Step out of the truck. Keep your hands in clear sight. Brace yourself against the bed of the truck and spread your legs."

"How come you're getting up my butt? I ain't done nothing."

"Assume the position."

Grumbling, Jackknife leaned against the car. He'd taken the trouble to clean up—probably hoping to impress Vi—and didn't look as disreputable as usual, despite the chaw of tobacco pushing out his cheek. Carter didn't actually think Jackknife was the serial killer, but the old man had been involved from the start. He patted him down, snapped on handcuffs and turned Jackknife around to face him.

"I have questions. If you answer correctly, you can go."

Jackknife nodded his head toward the building. "What about Vi? She said she was going to the FBI headquarters in Pueblo, and I wanna see her."

"Did she tell you she wanted to see you?"

"Maybe not. But I don't like her riding around with that other ranger guy."

"You drove around in circles before you dropped Daisy off near Butcher's Gulch. Why?"

"I was lost."

How dumb was this guy? He'd already admitted to taking a payoff. "Did someone pay you to make sure she didn't arrive until after dark?"

"I don't have to tell you."

"Suit yourself." Carter clamped his hand around Jackknife's upper arm, headed toward the FBI headquarters and started reciting the Miranda warning as if he intended to arrest the old man. "You have the right to remain silent. Anything you say—"

"Okay, stop right there. I'll talk," he said. "A punk kid showed up at my doorstep and gave me an envelope."

"What else?"

Inside were two $100 bills and instructions. If'n I drove Daisy around till after dark, I'd get another two bills." His mouth pulled down in a scowl. "I'm still waiting on the second half of the payoff."

"Why didn't you tell me this before? You never mentioned $100 bills."

"Because. I thought you'd take them away from me."

"Had you ever seen the kid before? Did you know the person who paid you?"

"That's a big, fat no."

His story didn't amount to proof but was very suggestive. Slade preferred to keep his money in cash, and Carter had seen Brandi pay for lunch with a $100 bill. If Jackknife had kept the payoff, they might be able to get prints. "Do you have either of the hundreds?"

"Hell, no. I already spent it." He stuck out his chest. "This here is a new jacket. I figured Vi would like it."

Carter believed Jackknife leaned toward a career of cheating, lying and petty scams. But was he a serial killer? Booking him at the local jail felt like a waste of time and effort. "Turn around and let me take the handcuffs off."

"You're cutting me loose?"

"With a warning. Until this serial killer is arrested, stay away from Daisy Brighton and her aunt Vi. If I catch you sniffing around again, you're going to jail for being a public nuisance."

He rubbed his wrists and gave Carter a sly grin. "See you around, Ranger."

"One more question. Did you really see Annie Brighton's grave at Butcher's Gulch?"

"The person who paid me gave me that hint." He shifted his tobacco from one side of his mouth to the other. "Maybe it was that Eric Wolff kid. He's always hanging around."

The pendulum swung back toward Eric. Which was it? Eric or Slade? Carter needed the answer before anyone else was killed.

Chapter Twenty-One

When Daisy strolled into the FBI offices with Carter, she immediately recognized the tension that came from having an outsider—her aunt Violet—who thought she knew better than everybody else because she'd watched every episode of a TV crime show. Though Vi's flirting had bewitched Joaquin, the other officers and agents had not succumbed.

Special Agent in Charge Pat Wiley pulled Daisy aside and said, "Your aunt is a busy little bee. She's tidied up stacks of filing, made fresh coffee, organized the condiments in the snack room and lectured me on the proper use of DNA evidence. She reminds me of my mom. I don't want to hurt her feelings, but—"

"I understand." Daisy empathized. "I might be able to convince her to come with me to explore the two major graveyards in the Pueblo area."

"Yes, please."

Should have been an easy solution, but Carter didn't want Daisy to go anywhere without him. He cornered her in the hallway by the elevator and spoke softly. "Another graveyard? I don't like this idea."

"Wiley loves it." She grinned. "I should go. I don't want to be in the way."

"In my mind, you're the center of this investigation. Everything revolves around you. And you are in danger." His blue eyes—periwinkle blue—pleaded with her. "Don't go."

"I don't want to hang around like an unnecessary appendage."

"A what?"

"An appendix." She chose a more appropriate comparison. "An organ that seems useless but can become infected and ruin everything."

"Not useless," he said firmly. "You're a lung or a liver."

"Or a pancreas?"

"Stay with me today." He glided his hand down her arm and took her hand, setting off a chain reaction of sizzling awareness. "Tonight, come home with me to my cabin."

Though his invitation wasn't specific, she understood exactly what he was proposing. As they stood in a public hallway where any number of people, including her aunt, could walk by, Carter drew an invisible curtain around them, shielding them from interruption. Tonight could be for them. Finally, they could lie together in his bed and make love.

She wanted that closeness, wanted to kiss him until her lips were bruised, to stroke her fingertips across his chest and to inhale his clean, masculine scent. No matter how irresponsible and impossible their relationship, she needed to join with him.

"I will come home with you tonight." Still, she

didn't capitulate. "For right now, I should go to the cemeteries with Aunt Vi. Joaquin will be with us. He'll keep us safe."

He brushed her cheek with a light kiss and whispered, "Until tonight."

She could hardly wait.

DAISY STOOD IN the main parking lot at Rolling Hills Cemetery south of Pueblo and waited for Joaquin to run around to the passenger side of his SUV to open the door for Vi. Before they left FBI headquarters, Daisy had checked the cemetery's registry for the 114,988 people who were buried on the nearly three hundred acres of manicured landscaping and statuary. According to the records, Elizabeth Franklin, Slade's mama, had a plot in a central area near the reflecting pool. Though she didn't know the first name of Hannah's uncle, there were several members of the Guerrero family. The most recently interred had a spot near Mama. Could that be how Slade met the young woman from Glenwood Springs? In spite of Eric's wall of stalking photos, she leaned more and more toward Slade.

Aunt Vi exhaled an impatient breath as she marched toward Daisy. "I don't know why we're wasting our time here."

Joaquin shuffled along behind her, his reluctance obvious. Like Carter, he preferred nature to human interaction, especially when the human—the lovely and somewhat irritating Violet Rhodes—thrived on conflict. She continued, "There's no record for Sherwood Brighton. Rolling Hills had barely been established when he died in 1896."

"I was thinking of Annie Brighton," Daisy said.

"His wife? But, sweetheart, you already found her grave in Butcher's Gulch." She glanced at Joaquin. "My niece is a genius in anatomy but sometimes forgets everyday details."

"Her burial site is important." Daisy reached into her backpack and found the letter from Annie to Morris Wolff that Eric had addressed to her. "Check out that line about taking the treasure to the grave."

Aunt Vi slipped on her silver-frame half glasses to read the sexy letter. She frowned and read it again. "Once again, it seems that our great-great-great-grandmother was a bit of a floozy, despite her renown as a seamstress of wedding dresses."

"There are a number of unmarked graves here," Daisy said. "And it occurs to me that Annie might have been buried under another name."

"Wolff?" Aunt Vi groaned. "I hope you aren't suggesting that she married that cur."

"It's worth a search as long as we're here." She looked toward Joaquin. "Am I right?"

He gazed toward the west, where the late-afternoon clouds had already begun to take on the pink and gold of sunset. "We've got one and half or two hours of good light. We should use it."

Daisy handed out maps she'd printed from the

online site and pointed them toward a section at the far southeast corner where tombstones with incomplete inscriptions—only a date or a first name—mingled with others. Vi charged toward that area while Joaquin and Daisy followed, strolling along a paved pathway. She continued to study the map, noticing that the grave of Slade's mother, Elizabeth Franklin, wasn't far from where they were walking.

This cemetery had an open, pleasant atmosphere. It was as friendly as a graveyard could be with plenty of visitors and groundkeepers. She felt safe enough to make a suggestion. "I want to make a quick stop. Why don't you catch up with Vi?"

"She's something else," he said as he watched her stride ahead of them. "Is she dating anyone else?"

"Second time this week someone's asked." And Joaquin Stanley ranked so much higher than Jackknife that they were hardly the same species. "At the moment, she's single."

"May I ask a personal question?"

"Go for it."

"How many former husbands?"

"Four. Two divorces and two deaths, including the love of her life. That was six years ago. She might be ready to get back into the game."

"Sounds reasonable."

Not wanting to interfere in this budding romance, she waved him on. "Keep going. Vi is waiting."

"And leave you by yourself? Hah! Carter would kill me."

"You can time me. This won't take more than five minutes."

"Just last night, you were being stalked."

Vi waved. "You two, hurry up."

"Go," Daisy said. "I'll be fine."

Reluctantly, he moved away from her as a group of ten or twelve mourners milled around them. "I'll be watching."

After consulting the map, she hurried along a pathway toward the central area, where she quickly found a square reflecting pool with a white marble statue of a praying angel with beautiful wings and flowing robes. In a quick moment, she found the white marble marker for Elizabeth Franklin. The epitaph said it all: "Gone but Never Forgotten. I Love You, Mama."

As Daisy reached out to touch the stone, she heard a voice. "Ever since the first time I saw you, walking alone and so serious, I imagined you here, close to Mama."

Slade loomed over her, gun in his hand. It was a huge weapon with an attachment on the barrel. She'd fallen into his trap. "What do you want?"

"If you make a sound, I'll kill your aunt and her ranger friend." He grasped her upper arm and yanked her away from the throng of mourners and closer toward him. "Come with me. Move fast."

When she stumbled, he poked the barrel of his gun into her ribs. "Quiet and fast."

She had no choice but to obey. When Vi and Joaquin were no longer in danger, she could deal with Slade. Maybe talk him into letting her go. Bide her time and find a way to escape.

Clearly, he knew his way around this cemetery. He dodged onto a narrow path that led between a mausoleum and a small chapel. No one—not Joaquin or Vi or any of the other people in the cemetery—could see them. Daisy hoped they wouldn't try to follow. But she heard Aunt Vi calling her name. If she and Joaquin ran toward the central area of the cemetery, Slade would have a clear shot—and he was a killer who wouldn't hesitate.

He slowed as they approached an open area with a low fence separating the cemetery grounds from a small parking area. Taking long strides, Slade dragged her forward. She heard her aunt shouting. Joaquin's voice joined hers.

A sob caught in Daisy's throat. Too late. *I'm going to die.* Should have stayed with Carter. Tonight they could have made love. Why did she wait?

At the parking lot, a man stepped out from behind a truck. Jackknife Jones had a gun of his own. He spit a wad of tobacco onto the asphalt. "You've got to be the guy who owes me two hundred bucks."

Slade cursed under his breath. "I don't know you."

"The hell you don't. I came to Pueblo to find you. Now gimme my money."

"Wasn't me."

"Then who?" His jaw dropped. "That Eric Wolff kid? It was him, wasn't it?"

Slade released his grasp on her, aimed and fired a handgun with a long tube attached to the barrel. A silencer? Jackknife went down.

Before Daisy could react, Slade pressed a stun gun against her neck. The painful shock of fifty thousand volts paralyzed her. She went unconscious.

NO POINT IN blaming each other. Or in rehashing what had happened and what they could have done differently. Joaquin and Vi had responded to the gunfire and witnessed enough of Slade's escape to say he'd headed west. They were on their way to FBI headquarters.

Carter went into action, charging into full-scale action, organizing an FBI task force dedicated to finding and arresting a serial killer. With authorization from SAC Wiley, he launched an aggressive police search for Slade's Toyota Corolla, using the license number on file. Following his suggestion, the FBI called in helicopters to scan the roads near Rolling Hills Cemetery.

Another possible source for information was Jackknife. Not dead. Not yet. An ambulance had taken him to the nearest hospital, where an ER nurse told Carter over the phone that he couldn't speak to the patient until after surgery. She'd also conveyed a message. Jackknife wanted to tell Carter he was sorry for lying. He thought the person who gave him two hundred bucks was Slade Franklin, but he was wrong. Eric Wolff, it was Eric.

Would it have made a difference if Carter had learned that information earlier? Eric was guilty of stalking Daisy, but Slade was a killer. He'd abducted her. Where the hell had he take her?

Agent Wiley picked his way through the cubicles and stepped up beside him. "I've got an off-road map and coordinates for Elizabeth Franklin's property near Lake Charlotte. A squad using a chopper can be there fast. To catch the bastard off guard."

"Do it."

Wiley gave him a thumbs-up and made a call.

Though Carter agreed with the plan, he didn't have a good feeling about Mama's cabin behind the No Trespassing sign. The location seemed too obvious, and Slade was as slippery as a weasel. If he felt them closing in, he'd dodge…and take Daisy with him.

When Wiley ended his call, Carter asked, "How fast can we get there?"

"We?" The veteran FBI agent combed his fingers through his thinning hair. His easygoing smile flattened into a stiff, straight line. "We aren't involved in this operation, Carter. This is a crack team from Fort Carson. They'll get him."

"I want to be there."

"Sorry." Wiley shrugged off Carter's concerns. "Leave this op to the experts. They're expert in hostage extraction."

It made a difference when the hostage was Daisy. They had to think of every detail. The cabin could be booby-trapped. An overeager squad member might discharge his weapon too soon. Was Daisy drugged? Wounded? Too many things could go wrong.

Before a tornado of doubt overwhelmed him, he paced away from Wiley and exited from FBI headquarters on the eighth floor. Through the floor-to-ceiling window at the far end of the hallway, he saw the last vivid orange and purple streaks of sunset. Nightfall didn't bode well for a search.

An hour and a half ago, he and Daisy had been standing close together outside the silver elevator door at the other end of the hall, talking about spending the night together. The ding of the arriving elevator startled him. When the door opened, Joaquin charged toward him, red-faced and out of breath. "Never should have taken my eyes off her."

"And I should have known better than to send her to the cemetery where his mama was buried. Slade knows his way around that place."

"Swear to God, it was only a minute."

"Not your fault," Carter said. "Not yours. Not mine. Not Wiley's. Not Daisy's. The only one to blame is Slade Franklin."

"Wise words." Joaquin nodded. "I'm the one who is trained to be a counselor, but you're catching on. Now, what can I do to help?"

"Come with me. We're going to visit a little old lady named Gallagher."

When they left in Joaquin's SUV, Carter phoned Wiley, told him that he was checking for other leads at Slade's house and asked him to report on the raid at the Lake Charlotte cabin. He looked over at Joaquin, who was making good time scooting through the streets of Pueblo at the tail end of rush hour. "Okay, counselor, give me the straight scoop on Slade."

"Narcissistic psychopath. Thinks he's smarter than everybody else. Has no moral filter to distinguish right from wrong."

"Why does he kill? Why these women?"

"I don't have enough information," he said. "Something to do with his mama."

Carter nodded, then changed the subject. "Where's Aunt Vi?"

"I was too distracted to watch her, so I contacted a local cop and arranged for him to drive her back to NPS headquarters in Salida. Travis can keep an eye on her until I get back."

"She could be in danger," Carter said. "I still don't trust Eric Wolff."

"Travis can handle it." Joaquin whipped into an illegal left turn and flew down a main road. "I like the lady. When this is over, I intend to take her to a steak house. You wouldn't think a dainty woman like Vi would go for a T-bone, but she loves beef. And carries a gun."

At this point, Daisy would have warned Joaquin about moving too fast with the much-married Aunt Vi. Thinking of her caused an ache in Carter's heart and an overwhelming need to bring her home safely.

Joaquin parked at the curb outside Slade's tidy yellow house with white trim, but Carter pointed him toward the neighbor's place. As before, Mrs. Gallagher answered the doorbell immediately. She smiled at Carter and peered through her extra-large glasses at Joaquin, scanning him from the top of his head to his size-thirteen boots.

"Well now," she said, "you're a big fella, aren't you?"

"Yes, ma'am."

"I'll bet you boys want some cookies."

Carter wanted information. Anything and everything she could tell him about the handsome, supposedly kindhearted son of her deceased friend Elizabeth… Slade Franklin, the serial killer next door.

Chapter Twenty-Two

A hoarse cough scraped the back of her throat. When she tried to swallow, the interior of her mouth felt dry and gummy. A headache stabbed between her eyebrows and penetrated all the way to the back of her skull, killing sensation and pinning her imaginary fears in place. How could she be afraid when confronted with all this reality, all this pain? Forcing herself to breathe, she inhaled sawdust and the sweet fragrance of lavender.

Daisy needed to waken but feared more agony. *Go back to sleep.* No. She couldn't quit. Not now. Nothing could hurt more than the full-body cramps twisting the muscles in her arms and legs into knots. Curled up on a long, wood bench, she cautiously tried to change positions. A soft cotton rope bound her wrists. Another linked her ankles. She was barefoot.

She opened her eyelids a slit and peered through the tears. In spite of many windows and a high, arched ceiling with open beams, the room held more shadows than light. Outside, night had fallen. Where was she? How long had she been asleep?

A soothing melody played on a discordant piano. "Moonlight Sonata" by Beethoven. She'd heard this music before. Recently. She poked her tongue through her lips, tried to swallow. So dry—her mouth was so dry.

She remembered. The first time she and Carter had visited Slade's house, he'd played the sonata. He must be here, plucking out the repetitive music on the keys. *He's here.* Now she was scared. She had to get away from him. Had to escape.

Struggling through the pain, she wriggled out from under the worn blanket covering her shoulders. She swung her legs down to the floor and sat upright on the first pew in a small sanctuary. The music surrounded her, choking off all other sounds.

Squinting, she sharpened her focus and saw a spinet piano beside a carved wood panel that separated the choir stalls from the altar, which was also lavishly decorated with a design of wheat and flowers. Slade's handiwork? Had he designed this place? For a homicidal psychopath, he was skilled.

And there he sat. Her captor. The man who would kill her.

Shoulders hunched, Slade continued to play the same notes over and over. He didn't seem to notice she was awake. This might be her best—maybe her only—chance to escape. Bent from the waist, she maneuvered her bound wrists so she could work on the knotted rope restraining her ankles. Unable to grip, her fingers were weak and clumsy. Her headache pounded mercilessly.

Slade abandoned the melody to hammer tunelessly on the keys. The harsh noise jolted.

"Daisy, Daisy," he sang. "Give me your answer, do."

Gritting her teeth, she tugged at the ropes. The loop around one ankle loosened. Would it be enough? Could she wiggle her bare foot and get free?

Slade rose to his full height, towering over the spinet. "Where are my manners? I should offer you a beverage. A glass of water?"

Sitting up and hoping he wouldn't look at her ankles, she tried to respond but could only manage a few garbled syllables.

"What was that?" he asked. "You want a clear rum like the stuff Brandi gave you? Oh, I don't think so. Mama wouldn't approve."

"Wa-wa-water."

"Much better."

With a dramatic flourish that didn't match his outfit of jeans, flannel shirt and work boots, he pivoted and strode through a door behind the choir stalls. Now was her chance.

She inhaled a deep breath, pushed her foot free from the rope and attempted to stand. For a terrifying moment, she balanced on the razor edge of equilibrium. *Don't fall. Don't fall.* Her mind spun out of control, shattering her vision into a kaleidoscope. Into the past, the present and the unknown future. *Can't move.* Hopeless, she sank down onto the pew. Her eyes snapped shut, and she embraced the familiar darkness. *Think. Use your head.*

She remembered the autopsy suite and Dr. Julia's calm, nurturing voice as she listed the combination of drugs Slade had used on prior victims to control them. First, he hit them with a stun gun to immediately disable their natural reactions. Then came the parade of sedatives, most of which were designed to wear off quickly.

When she twisted to the left, she felt a possible spot where he had administered a hypodermic—using the same technique he'd used on Andrea. When he appeared again in the sanctuary, it felt like she'd been waiting for an hour. But it had probably only been a minute or two. After congratulating herself on making sense of her drugged reactions, she tried a nonthreatening smile to let him know she'd cooperate.

He held the water glass to her mouth. "Small sips. Don't want you to glug it and vomit."

Hoping desperately that he hadn't put a drug in the water, she tasted. The cool liquid moistened her lips. Instant relief lifted her spirits. She tried to speak again. "Head hurts."

He held the glass for her again. "You're going to be fine, aren't you? You're a strong one. I saw that in you at the first glimpse."

"When was that?"

"Butcher's Gulch. Don't you remember. You had just found Rene."

Of course she remembered. But if that was the first time he'd seen her, he couldn't have arranged with Jackknife to drive in circles. It didn't make sense, not unless the payoff came from Eric Wolff.

After he placed the water glass on the floor, he sat beside her and dug a vial of pain relievers from his pocket. He tapped out three. "Wash these down with water."

Reminding herself that none of his victims had been raped or shown signs of torture, she didn't fight him. But there was no way she trusted him enough to take his meds. "I'm okay."

He ran his large hand over his bristly, buzz-cut hair. "We both like graveyards, you and me. Such peaceful places, even those that aren't landscaped or as well maintained as Rolling Hills. I knew you'd go there sooner or later."

She tried to nod, but the motion proved too difficult. Her head lolled forward before she regained her balance. "Reflecting pool."

"It's pretty, isn't it? I knew Mama would enjoy having a plot close to the center of the cemetery. It took some masterful negotiating to get that space for her, but I persevered."

"You're a good son." She chose her words deliberately, expecting that he wanted to hear how much his mama cared about him. "She loved you."

"But I still haven't made her happy." He frowned. "Mama wanted me to find the perfect mate, someone who could clean my house and cook and take care of me. Are you that girl, Daisy?"

Hell, no. She didn't speak. Just nodded.

"I brought a pretty yellow scarf for you, just like the kind Mama wears. But I lost it."

When he was hiding outside Carter's cabin. "Do you have another?"

"Six or seven. Maybe I don't need to get more. Maybe you're the girl I'm looking for. Should we go into the kitchen and see how well you can cook?"

The fog in her brain had begun to dissipate. If she could convince him to take her into the kitchen, dozens of weapons—knives, boiling water, heavy fry pans—would be close at hand. Before she attempted her escape, she had to be able to run. When she flexed the quadriceps in her upper thigh, the muscles trembled. Not ready for action.

"I'll cook for you." She stammered. "W-w-what's your favorite food?"

"Mac and cheese, made from scratch with cheddar and gouda." He stretched his long legs straight out in front of him. "I was going to make some later. I've got all the ingredients, even the cheese, in the kitchen behind the rec room."

"Where are we?"

"The Nature Chapel of DSC, which stands for Divine Spirit Church." He looked around with a proprietary air. "I did most of the wood finishing in here. Now I'm renovating the kitchen. The pastor and the board had me submit a bid. As if there was any doubt? They hired me on the spot. I do good work."

That must have been his evening appointment

after she and Carter visited him and Brandi. "You worked for them before?"

"Sure have. DSC is Mama's church." He scowled. "Your FBI buddies made my life difficult when they confiscated my truck. I couldn't bring all my supplies."

She didn't want him to be angry at her. "Not me."

"I know that, Daisy." He slid the back of his hand down her cheek, and she held herself very still to keep from flinching away from him. "You're a good girl. I don't like Ranger Carter."

Hearing his name spoken by this murderer disgusted her. Carter was such a good person, moral and strong and so damn handsome. Thinking of him, believing that she would see him again, gave her strength.

Slade gazed toward the altar, and his dark eyes softened. "I remember Andrea Lindstrom. A very good cook."

He'd held on to Andrea for an extra three days. Hadn't brought her here because he didn't have the job until a day ago. His lair? "Was she the sort of woman Mama would like?"

"Very much so. With her blond hair, she looked like you."

Not really. Andrea had had platinum hair, while Daisy's curls were streaked and honey blond. Still, she nodded. "I guess so."

"We were happy, me and Andrea. Then she tried to run away from me."

"Were you at your house in town?"

He gave her a suspicious look. "Why do you want to know?"

"Curious." She had to be careful. If he thought she was investigating him, he'd clam up—or, more likely, he'd decide she wasn't worth the risk and kill her. "Because Brandi is so jealous."

"Yeah, she is." He chuckled. "I took Andrea to a little cabin that Mama left to me. Very secluded. Private. Maybe you and I can go there."

She flexed her quads again and felt the strength returning to her muscles. Supposedly, Slade liked the cabin, but he hadn't taken Rene to his lair. And he'd killed Hannah on the spot at Doc Holliday's tomb. She wondered about Eileen Findlay, the Ute woman. "Did you take anybody else to Mama's cabin?"

"Too many questions," he said. "All you really need to know is how to take care of me the way Mama did."

"Can't help it." She managed to raise and lower her shoulders in a shrug. "I ask questions. I'm a scientist."

"Okay, Miss Scientist. You can ask one question. Only one."

Her investigation with Carter had answered many of the mysteries surrounding the serial murders, but they'd never understood the motivation. Knowing full well that the profile for a serial killer wouldn't fit the parameters of logic, she still wanted to hear what he had to say. "Why me?" She asked, "Why any of us, but mostly, why did you choose me?"

He stood and went to the low altar rail, which was carved and sanded to match the other wood in the sanctuary. Slowly, he paced from one end to the other with measured steps. "You probably won't understand."

Try me, you narcissistic creep. "I'll try."

"About a year after Mama died, my grief became so intense that I wanted to lie down in the grave beside her and end the torture of loneliness. I knelt by her grave, waiting for a sign, and I saw a young woman, also in pain about the death of a loved one. We wept in each other's arms."

She couldn't feel sorry for Slade. Not when she knew this tender story ended in murder. "What was her name?"

"No more questions." He resumed his pacing. "I took her to Mama's cabin near Lake Charlotte. She stayed with me, cleaned my house, cooked for me. After a few days, she wanted to go home, to return to her family. I couldn't let her leave me."

And so, he killed her. Adrenaline rushed through her bloodstream, counteracting the influence of the drugs he'd given her. She said nothing.

He continued to pace and to talk. "I took her to Rolling Hills after dark to give her one more opportunity to say she'd stay. She didn't. I squeezed her neck until she stopped moving and laid her beside the grave of her loved one."

Pivoting, he faced Daisy. "That woman broke my heart. I waited by her body until dawn, when another woman came to the cemetery. That was when I knew."

Knew what? With the obvious questions burning in her throat, she waited.

"The woman who found the body was meant to be my mate," he said. "Mama sent her to me. That's how I've found all of you."

So random. And yet so specific. He had selected his victims based on who found the body. Eileen Findlay, killed in Riverwalk Park, was found by Hannah Guerrero, who was found by Andrea Lindstrom, who was found by Rene Williams. And now it was Daisy's turn. She had found Rene's body. This was her fate.

WITH TENSION RISING, Carter urged Joaquin to drive faster. He had to reach Daisy and know that she was all right. The narrow road leading to the Nature Chapel of the Divine Spirit Church was rutted, narrow and didn't look like it went anywhere. "Are you sure this is the right way?"

"I've been here before," Joaquin said. "I give lectures at local churches about fire safety and pass out souvenirs to the kids."

The road was so narrow that tree branches

brushed against the passenger door. “This is too remote for a church.”

“DSC has a huge congregation in Pueblo, but this chapel is only used for retreats and special events, like marriages and anniversaries.”

“And abductions?”

Joaquin took his eyes off the road for a moment and shot him a meaningful look. “You care about her. I can see it. You’ve only been together a few days, but there’s a connection.”

Carter didn’t bother denying their relationship. In addition to his education and training as a counselor, Joaquin was one of his best friends. “Damn right, I care. If he hurts her—”

“Don’t go there. We’ll stop him. We’re lucky to have found this lead.”

Luck had very little to do with it. Carter had been operating on a logical basis when he looked up Mrs. Gallagher. After she served “the boys” a plateful of snickerdoodles, she’d mentioned that her neighbor Slade—one of her favorite people—had a renovation job at the chapel and wouldn’t be home until late. Moments later, Joaquin and Carter had set their destination.

During their drive into the forest, SAC Wiley kept them updated on the speakerphone about the progress of the hostage extraction squad from Fort Carson. Their approach to the little cabin near Lake Charlotte sounded like an action-adventure movie with choppers making strategic landings, surveillance from drones, heat-sensing equipment and flash-bangs.

After one particularly dramatic report, Joaquin said, “I’m feeling underequipped.”

“Not me.” Carter stared into the night. “I could tear this guy apart with my bare hands.”

Joaquin pulled off onto a wide shoulder of the road. “We’re here.”

The Nature Chapel was about fifty yards from where they’d parked. Through the tree trunks of a pine forest, Carter saw lights from a square, white clapboard building with a short, fat steeple and a cross on top. An attached structure had a row of windows with no lights showing.

Carter heard a piano playing “Moonlight Sonata”—Slade’s favorite melody.

From the speaker, he heard Wiley’s report about the property at Lake Charlotte . “They broke into the cabin. Nice, neat parlor. Functional kitchen. On the dining table, he has an array of cutting and whittling tools. One of the closets is full of long, silky scarves. There’s blood on the floor. This is the place. The serial killer’s lair. But I’m sorry, Carter. He’s not there.”

“I know.”

“How?”

“I’m listening to him play the piano.”

While Joaquin gave SAC Wiley directions to the Nature Chapel, Carter dodged through the trees.

As he approached the chapel, the music fell silent. Something was happening.

In the long, flat-topped building attached to the chapel, lights went on. Holding his Beretta at the ready, Carter got close and peered through one of the dirty windows. Slade chattered mindlessly as he helped Daisy walk through a casual gathering area that seemed to be a rec room. Her unfastened hair fell around her face, her gait was stumbling and she was shoeless. A soft, gray rope bound her wrists. She appeared to be unharmed.

While Slade escorted her around an open counter into a kitchen, Joaquin stepped up beside Carter. He gestured toward the end of the long building, and Carter nodded agreement. Ducking low so they wouldn't be seen through the windows, they moved to the end of the building. Carter turned the handle on a simple wood door. Unlocked.

"Inside, we split up," Carter whispered. "We go to the kitchen."

"I'll take the far door. You take the closer."

They slipped into the rec room and made their way across a checkerboard pattern of green and red tiles—Christmas colors. At the end closest to the door was a three-foot-tall stage with a curtain. Several long, collapsible tables were arrayed on the floor.

He heard Slade talking about how Mama made the best mac and cheese. "You've got to boil the pasta until it's soft."

"Sure," Daisy said. "I can't cook unless you untie my hands."

"Well, I guess that makes sense."

When he did as she asked, Carter was proud of her. Smart move. He eased around the counter into the kitchen, which was, apparently, where most of the renovation work was being done. On the countertop near the sink, he saw an electric handsaw and a nail gun. Hammers, chisels, screwdrivers and other tools littered the other surfaces.

"Do you have any bacon?" Daisy asked. "I like to crumble some on top."

"I suppose we can try it, but that's not what Mama did." Slade took the bacon from the double-wide refrigerator and laid it on the counter beside her. "Anything else?"

"Frying pan," she said.

He lifted a cast iron skillet from under the counter and placed it on the burner. Carter could tell from the way Daisy looked at the pan that she was considering using it as a weapon. He needed to act fast, to gain control. He stepped around the center island and aimed his Beretta.

"Freeze," Carter shouted. "Police."

From the opposite side, Joaquin echoed the warning.

Slade ignored both of them. He bolted toward the counter, picked up the nail gun. Before he could shoot, Daisy stepped up with the cast iron skillet and whacked him on the side of the head. Slade went down.

Half collapsing, Daisy almost followed him to the floor. But Carter caught her and held her close. He nuzzled her hair, kissed her forehead.

"You found me," she said.

"And I'm never going to let you go."

After Joaquin secured the cuffs on Slade and put through a call to SAC Wiley, he turned toward them. "I'm sorry, Daisy. I did a lousy job of taking care of you."

"Not your fault."

Carter guided her away from the rec room and into the adjoining sanctuary. So many things he wanted to tell her. So many promises he longed to make.

He seated her in the first pew facing the altar and went down on one knee in front of her.

Alarm crossed her face. "No," she said.

"You haven't heard what I'm going to say."

"Better not be a marriage proposal."

He took her hand. "Daisy Brighton, I want more time with you. I don't know how long. Days, weeks, maybe a lifetime. Will you promise to spend time with me?"

"I will."

And then they kissed.

Epilogue

Three months later, in September, before the first big snowfall, Daisy had started teaching science at the high school in Buena Vista, which was halfway between Leadville and Salida. Though she maintained her own apartment near the school, she spent a lot of time at Carter's cabin. On this particular Saturday morning, she stood in front of the clothes she'd hung in his closet, trying to make up her mind.

When he entered the bedroom, wearing only his black jersey boxers and his cowboy hat, she asked, "What's the appropriate outfit for an exhumation?"

"I don't think the dead will care." He set a steaming mug of coffee on the bedside table and slipped up behind her for a hug and a nibble on her earlobe. "You'd better decide quick. We've got to get rolling."

She took a swallow of rich coffee, turned to face him and groaned with pleasure. The taste was great. Looking at him was even better. She loved the way the morning light from the dormer outlined his muscular shoulders and the sprinkle of soft black hair that arrowed down his chest. "Do we have time for a shower?"

"We do. Wouldn't want you to turn up at Butcher's Gulch all dirty and stinky."

"I'm never stinky."

"After a day in autopsy with Dr. Julia, you're not exactly a bouquet of roses."

Taking a shower together saved water and was always a treat, even on mornings like this when they had to rush through the soaping, rinsing and naked groping. It had taken a long time for them to decide to make love, but once that switch was turned, they couldn't keep their hands off each other.

Stepping from the shower, she wrapped herself in a fluffy yellow towel, dashed into the bedroom and selected a forest green pantsuit—practical, sensible and respectful. She'd worn this outfit often during the trial of Slade Franklin. His insanity plea failed, despite evidence to the contrary, and he was found guilty of at least four murders and sentenced to life in prison. Brandi did live interviews during the trial, and her vlog became even more popular.

Daisy jumped into Carter's SUV, and they drove to Butcher's Gulch. This morning, Aunt Vi had arranged for the exhumation of the grave of Annie Brighton.

Though Daisy and Carter were early, a crowd had already gathered. Aunt Vi and Joaquin Stanley led the pack, and she was supervising three men with shovels who were digging into the soil of boot hill. Jackknife Jones—fully recovered—waved to Daisy and then spit tobacco juice on a nearby grave. She wasn't happy to see Gerald Wolff and his son, Eric, who had put together that stalker's wall that he explained to the police was only an artistic expression of his search for the bullion. He also admitted to paying Jackknife as a prank, a sick joke on Daisy.

After greeting Aunt Vi with a kiss and hugging Joaquin, she took Carter's hand and leaned toward him. In a whisper, she asked, "Isn't there something you can arrest one or both of the Wolff men for?"

"No law against being a jerk."

"When we find something," Aunt Vi said, "we promised to give them twenty-five percent."

"If we find something," Daisy said.

They watched while the hired men dug. Aunt Vi had gone to a lot of trouble to obtain proper paperwork, even though the boot hill wasn't owned or supervised by anyone. If they found anything... there was a question of ownership. The loot had been stolen, after all.

One of the shovels made a heavy clunk as it hit a solid surface. The coffin. In minutes the plain wood box was uncovered.

In spite of herself, Daisy was excited.

The lid was torn off. A sheet removed. Inside the coffin, packed from one end to another, was gold bullion—the treasure Annie Brighton had taken to the grave.

* * * * *